-THE-
SUN SINGER

COTI DE LAINE

Copyright © Coti De Laine 2024
All rights reserved.

No part of this publication may be altered, reproduced, distributed, or transmitted in any form, by any means, including, but not limited to, scanning, duplicating, uploading, hosting, distributing, or reselling, without the express prior written permission of the publisher, except in the case of reasonable quotations in features such as reviews, interviews, and certain other non-commercial uses currently permitted by copyright law.

Disclaimer:
This is a work of fiction. Some characters, locations, and businesses are purely products of the author's imagination and used fictitiously. Any resemblance to actual people, living or dead, or to businesses, places, or events is completely coincidental.

"But when the Son of Man returns, will he find faith on the earth?"
—*Luke 18:8*

ONE
DENIM GUY

Jenin Refugee Camp
June 16th, 2035

I'M NOT A PRAYING man, not anymore. When Vivian passed, I swore I'd never ask God for another thing. But as I stare at my son's weakening vital signs beamed to my phone through an app, I must admit, I'm tempted to pray ... and to ask.

"We almost there," says the cab driver in broken English. His name is Ameen. He flashes a gold-toothed grin and points his finger out the window. "Not long now. You see."

The phone goes back into my pocket as the maroon Mazda bounces down a cramped street. The hum of the motor with no muffler drowns out the noise outside. My guide from the UNRWA, a silver-haired sanitation worker named Ibrahim, sits next to me. He cranes his neck to look out the dusty windshield.

"Look, if he isn't here then I'm going home," I say to Ibrahim. "Back to the US." Chasing down this story has already made me look foolish to my colleagues, but that isn't why I want to go home. Sam needs me. What am I doing here?

Ibrahim pats my leg. "He will be here Ethan. This time, he will be here."

This time was the twelfth refugee camp we had visited in the last two weeks in an attempt to find the elusive "Forever Man." Through an anonymous tip to the *New York Times*, I find myself on the other side of the world, looking for a supposed miracle worker and do-gooder who goes by the name of Yeshua. This is not just any Yeshua. The locals say this is THE Yeshua. Jesus of Nazareth. The one the Christians worship. It sounds crazy because it is crazy. But this Yeshua has no social media accounts, no press, no online presence, no documents, nothing to say that he exists other than rumors. Oh, and billions of followers, that is, if he really is Jesus of Nazareth.

Ameen slams on the brakes and my head hits the front headrest. When the dust clears, I see a bunch of people crowded around one of the numerous dwellings that are stacked on top of each other in the Jenin Camp.

"We're here," says Ameen rubbing his fingers together.

I hand him the money for the ride and hop out of the car. Plumes of dust hit my face along with a blast of searing heat. Squinting, I try to make out the cause of all the commotion.

Men, women, and children stand around speaking in Arabic. Emaciated dogs run through the crowd panting and sniffing for food. Something certainly has everyone excited.

Ibrahim begins speaking in Arabic to a few bystanders. Everyone seems confused. More kids are running around playing. My guide works his way through the crowd, apparently trying to piece together what's going on. I wait by the street and decide to clean off my sunglasses.

Eventually, I'm motioned to enter the house. I offer apologies as I push past a few onlookers. They look up, startled to see a random white guy in their midst. Near the doorway, I move to the side as one of the Palestinian workers, a man in a denim snap-button shirt, carries out a bucket of wastewater. The smell is horrendous, but out of a desire not to offend, I refrain from covering my nose.

Inside the building, it's cramped and not very well lit. Ibrahim is speaking with an elderly woman in a black hijab. I walk over to where they are standing. The woman is talking fast, gesturing with her hands. Ibrahim is nodding.

During a break in the dialogue, he turns to me. "OK, Ethan ..."

The woman starts talking again, pointing toward the sink. Ibrahim pauses to listen.

More head-nodding.

"All right," Ibrahim dabs his forehead with a handkerchief. "Apparently there was a sewage pipe burst. But they are fixing it. And good news! She says The Forever Man is here."

I take off my sunglasses. "The Forever Man? Is she certain?"

"The Forever Man," Ibrahim confirms. "Yes, that's what the Palestinians call him here."

"Good." I get out my pen and pad. "So, um, where exactly is he, the uh, Forever Man?"

"She said he has a denim blue shirt on."

"A denim shirt?" I put on my reading glasses. I look around the room. "The only person I saw with a denim shirt was one of the repair workers."

Ibrahim converses with the woman again. She points to the door, through which comes the same man, arms, and shirt splattered with brown wastewater. His sleeves are rolled up, and he's focused on the task at hand.

Ibrahim shrugs. "She says he's the one."

I point to the worker in exasperation. "Him?" Ibrahim nods.

The denim worker walks past me, grabs a wrench from a toolbox, and starts cranking on a pipe below the sink. He's about 5'9½", maybe 5'10", slender build, short-trimmed beard, and medium-long dark hair. There was nothing remarkable about him. Nothing that would say "I'm the savior of the world." In fact, he was so nondescript I walked right by him and didn't take much notice of the diminutive man. On his back, he cranks on the pipe some more. He motions with his hand, says something in Arabic.

"Turn the water on," Ibrahim translates to me.

I snap out of my dazed shock and open the tap to the sink. Clear water pours out. The woman claps and shouts in joy. The crowd outside celebrates. Denim Guy—that's what I'll call him for now—gets up from the floor. The woman grabs his head. She kisses his cheeks like the man is her long-lost son. For the next hour, the locals gathered outside come up to thank him, patting him on the back. He speaks to each one as if they were the only person in the world that ever existed. Whomever this guy is, he is loved.

Outside, the sun is getting low. By the time the crowd clears, my stomach is growling, and my feet are hurting. But I must admit that I am transfixed by what I have just witnessed. I see Ibrahim finally getting a chance to speak to Denim Guy. He looks over at me. For the first time, I sense something different about this man. He's sweaty, dirty, nondescript, normal, and ... extraordinary. I realize now that it's the eyes. Brown in color, they were at the same time mysterious and familiar. When he saw me, I felt immediately uncomfortable, like I was exposed, as if he could see everything about me.

Denim Guy nods his head. He and Ibrahim walk over to where I'm standing.

"This is Ethan Tellinger," says Ibrahim with his hand out. "The reporter from the *New York Times*."

"Hello Ethan," says Denim Guy. "Nice to meet you." He holds out his hand, then realizes it's dirty, so he waves to me instead.

"Hi there, would you have time for a few questions?"

"Of course. Let's talk on my way home. I don't live very far from here." Denim Guy speaks perfect English but with a heavy Middle Eastern accent.

After a quick clean up, I and Denim Guy chat a little as we make our way through the narrow streets. Ibrahim follows behind. We talk about the camp, my background, food, a few other ice-breaker topics. Although he seems normal, I can't shake the feeling of being completely captivated by this unimposing man. I ask if I can memorialize what he says as being on the record.

"Sure," was his direct response. Usually, people get weirded out when I ask this question, but Denim Guy seems like the most laid-back person I have ever met. We cross a parking lot and I press the red button on my recorder. At some point, I need to work up the nerve to ask *the question*. I don't know how to broach the subject delicately, so I just blurt it out.

"So, are you *him*?"

Denim Guy folds his hands behind his back. "Him?"

"Yes, uh, um, Yeshua … Jesus of Nazareth. Jesus the Christ. The Head of the Church, and all that."

"Ah. I never told anyone I was Jesus."

I feel a sense of relief. Maybe even some disappointment, but I appreciate his honesty. It appears this was just going to be another human-interest story for the *Times*. Maybe a feel-good story. My editor would like that.

"Nevertheless," he continues. "Some people recognize me."

"Wait." I stop walking and turn to face Denim Guy directly.

"You're saying you ARE him?"

He shrugs. "The people who know me, recognize me. I don't have to tell them who I am. They know."

"Oh, well. OK then." I scratch my head. "In that case, when were you born?"

"2,037 years ago."

Again, the direct specificity of the answer catches me off guard.

Clearly, this man is insane.

"And you've been living in a refugee camp ever since …?"

"No, no. Until recently I was still at the right hand of the Father in heaven, well, I still am I suppose, in a way. But a year ago my father determined the time had come, so I returned to earth in the flesh, just as I said I would."

"Ah, right. Yeah, um … yeah."

Ibrahim grabs my shoulder. "I must return to my family. Will you be good here?"

"I'll make sure he comes back in one piece," says Denim Guy. Suddenly aware of the time, I look at my watch. "Are you sure …?"

"It's fine," he says. "Go to your family, Ibrahim."

I thank my guide for his help, and he departs back the way we came.

Denim Guy kneels to pet one of the stray dogs. "You seem perplexed, Ethan Tellinger."

"Well, I'm not sure what people will say when I tell them that the Second Coming of Christ has occurred, but no one noticed, and that Jesus has been living in a Palestinian refugee camp."

Denim Guy grins. "I know what they will say. They will say you are crazy."

I let out a chuckle. "Right."

Denim Guy—or should I say Jesus?—takes a deep breath. "This is where I feel the most welcome on earth. In refugee camps, hospitals, prisons, all the places where people don't want to go, that is where you will find me and my followers. After over 2,000 years I came back because my father willed it to be so. And now? Now I will never leave again. The time has come for God to live with mankind in the physical realm. No more walls, no more curtains. No more physical separation. In spirit and truth, I have been with my followers always. Now I will be with everyone in the flesh."

I clear my throat. "About that. Pardon my ignorance. But wasn't there supposed to be a little more fanfare with your return? Your followers talk about there being clouds of glory and angels and … well, you know … the whole thing."

"Yes, all of that happened, but again, no one noticed." Denim Guy stands up and starts walking again. "No one was there when I walked out of the tomb all those years ago, even though I told them I would. I walked out and no one was there. So why would anyone notice when I returned? I even said I would return, several times! Then I had John write it down in a book. People are finite, they have a short memory, even my followers have stopped expecting my return, so when I finally did return, they didn't notice."

He takes a turn up a narrow alley. Decrepit buildings teeter overhead to each side. Clothes and towels attached to lines flap in the breeze between the houses. After a few yards, he ducks his head through a blue tarp. He lifts it open for me to enter. "Welcome to my home."

The *home* is more like a canvas shack, sandwiched in between two buildings. There is only one room, about ten feet by ten feet. There's a water spigot in the corner, a shelf with a few books, a sleeping mat on the dirt floor. An extension cord connects a portable electric stove. Denim Guy turns it on to heat a camping kettle.

Not sure where to stand, I decide to sit on the ground. "Hardly the dwelling for the King of Kings, wouldn't you say?"

Denim Guy laughs. "You should have seen where I was born." He pours a hot liquid into a plastic cup and hands it to me. "Have some tea."

"Right. Thank you." I take a sip, wondering if it will be the best tea ever, but no, it just tastes like normal tea. "So, if you don't mind, maybe I could circle back to something you said about your followers only being found in needy places. I would think that at least some of them, maybe most of them, would be in churches, no?"

Denim Guy sits next to me. "Wherever people are gathered in my name, I am there with them. But I go where I am needed. Where I am needed, there you will find my followers, and there you will find me."

"I'm not sure I understand."

He rubs his beard, and his eyes drift upward. "If I asked you to go find a monkey, where would you go?"

"The zoo."

Denim Guy raises an eyebrow. "Not the jungle? Most monkeys are in the jungle, Ethan Tellinger."

"Yes, but it's easier to find one at the zoo, even though, I suppose there are fewer of them there."

He nods his head. "You have spoken truly. Fewer still are kept as pets, but it doesn't make sense to go knocking on people's doors, trying to find which one has a pet monkey! This would be a terrible use of one's time, no?"

I set down my tea. "I see. So, visibility is not an indicator of quantity. I suppose that makes sense, but are you saying most of your followers aren't in churches?"

"Not necessarily. I have known many criminals who were closer to the Kingdom of Heaven than many pastors. The truth is that not many people *can* follow me. Not many can go where I go. Those who think they can, usually can not. Those few who know they are not able to follow are the ones who end up being called my disciples. And still, those who think they are my disciples, sometimes are not. Many think they can follow me, but it is a difficult way, a narrow way …"

"Yes, the uh, the small gate." I fumble around in my bag for my phone, then realize it's still in my pocket. "Right, I think I remember from Sunday school … The Gospel of Matthew? Chapter 7 …"

"Right! The small gate, which means you must *be* small to enter. The ego has no place in my Kingdom. Many cannot enter the small gate because they cannot be small. It is a great gift to be able to become small. Only the Spirit can give this gift of grace. Without it, people cannot enter the gate. Why? They cannot be weak, and they would never allow their weakness to be weak enough to proceed through. One of life's great questions is whether a person's weakness is weak enough, and not, as it were, whether their strength is strong enough. Most people want to be strong, self-reliant. I search for poverty of spirit. Where there is poverty, I find my followers. Where there is prosperity, it is harder to find my disciples. That is why I have fewer followers in the West."

"You mean the Bible-thumpers, and TV preachers? Evangelicals?"

He waves a dismissive hand and takes a sip of tea. I'm not sure how to interpret the gesture.

"And the Palestinians here, are they your followers?" I ask.

"A very small portion, yes, here and there. There are always some, even in the most hostile places. I know them by name." Denim Guy begins to prepare a bowl of rice. "Mostly, I just like to be with them, the Palestinians that is. I like to be with the poor and destitute, the downtrodden, the marginalized, the displaced. I like to be with sinners, and people who don't like me. I like to be close enough to my enemies that I can serve them."

Together we share a single bowl of rice. There's no salt or soy sauce. To my Western palate, it's like eating a tasteless kind of matter.

"On that note, talk about sinners. What exactly is a sinner?" "A sinner is a human."

"But, I mean …" The recorder starts beeping. "Hold on." I change out the batteries. Denim Guy sips his tea and waits patiently. "OK, you were saying …"

"All have sinned. And people are free to choose how they exist. I would hope they choose to exist with me, but they don't have to."

"But aren't you …" "Human?" He smiles.

"Right. I'm sorry, I'm not a theologian."

Denim Guy cracks a smile. "I'm all human, and all God." "Hm, OK. So, 100% human and 100% God. Got it."

He shakes his head. "No, no, that's not right. That's a contradiction. It's better to say that I am *fully* God, and *fully* human. A sinless human. The first."

"Got it. I think." I set down my bowl and stifle a yawn.

"Yes, it's getting late," Denim Guy says. "Why don't you stay here with me in my hut."

"Oh, I uh, um, all right." My mind races, trying to figure out the logistics. I'm not sure how to respond. Yet again Denim Guy catches me by surprise. He offers a hand and helps me to my feet. "Well, I guess, if it's not too inconvenient. I do have some more questions."

"Have no fear, Ethan Tellinger. DENIM GUY will answer all your questions."

At first, I don't notice what he said, but then I freeze. I feel my heart pound, and the blood drains out of my face. "Wait, how … how did you?" I drop my bag and stumble backward. I've always thought myself to be a practical person, but … is this really happening? Did this guy, this Denim Guy, really read my mind? I always thought supernatural stuff was crazy. I'm a rational person. I deal with facts. I believe in science.

Denim Guy steadies me. "I believe in science too," he says. Uh oh. Nope. The hut spins.

"It's all right, my friend. Let's set you down."

Gingerly, I'm helped to the ground. There's an arm there to catch me. Denim Guy is smiling down at me, a compassionate look on his face, and I wonder.

Could this be the face of ... *Jesus?*

TWO
A LESSON IN BUNGI-TIME

"I HAVE TO ASK, why do they call you The Forever Man?"

I sip my black tea, then munch on some flatbread retrieved by Denim Guy sometime in the night. It's the morning of the next day, and though my back is sore, I'm surprised to have slept reasonably well.

"Oh, that's kind of an inside joke with the people here," says Denim Guy. "If you stick around me long enough, you'll understand."

"Hm. All right."

"Well, what do you want to ask me today, Ethan Tellinger?" Denim Guy sits on the ground next to me and crosses his legs.

I clear my throat and get my recorder. "Yes, um, so ... I don't know how to explain last night. Maybe you can read minds? But claiming to be God is something else altogether."

"Agreed."

"When you say you are Jesus Christ, the Son of God, you are saying you created the dirt we are sitting on."

"I did," Denim Guy says with a matter-of-fact tone.

"Not just the dirt, but everything, right? The whole world, the animals, plants."

He nods his head. "The whole universe."

"Sure. All of it, created by ... you."

Denim Guy sets down his tea and leans back on his elbow. "By me and *through* me, and for me. Every sub-atomic particle and microscopic bacteria. Even the universe's mathematical framework. All me."

"A dude living in a tent."

He shakes his head emphatically. "No, no. That's not correct. Not at all." He looks around. "This is not a tent. It's more like a lean-to."

Denim Guy cracks a smile.

I smile back. "Good one. OK, a dude in a lean-to. But what about time? Did you create time? Are you in time, or outside of time? Timeless? Explain how that works."

Calloused, scarred hands run through his hair. "Yes, in a sense I created time, at least as you experience it. But it's not quite right to say that I am outside time or inside time, or timeless. More accurately, I exist *upon* time."

"I'm sorry, you lost me there."

Denim Guy rubs his chin and stares off into the distance. "In this dimension time is like a train, constantly moving from one sequential event to another. Humanity and the physical world, they are like passengers with a ticket that says they can only move around in their assigned car. But me? I'm like the conductor. I can go outside the train. I can stop the train. I can speed up the train. I can move between cars. I can go all the way to the front and see what's ahead. I can go all the way to the back and see what's behind. I can climb outside and walk on the roof. I can slow the train to a crawl and go for a walk on the ground outside. For you, the train keeps moving like always. You can look outside the window and notice it's slowed down based on your speed. For me, I can spend a lot of *'time'* outside the train. You see, it's not that I am in time, but that I can choose to move WITH time as I exist upon it."

Pretty sure I didn't understand any of that, but I go along. "So, as for me ... I'm *trapped* in time?"

"In a sense, yes, for now, at least." "And what does that mean?" I ask.

"Before, right now, not yet. These tensed concepts keep you trapped in time. But the train had to start somewhere. If it's moving, then it's going somewhere too. Would you believe it if I told you that time itself longs to find its final resting place? Only in me …" Denim Guy trails off. He looks at me with a raised eyebrow. "You think I'm crazy right?"

"Well …" I search for some other word besides *crazy*, but nothing comes to mind. "Anyways, um, going back to the start of the train, before that, what was happening? What existed, or what kind of existence was there?"

Now Denim Guy is laughing and shaking his head. "You don't even believe I created all this," he says, spreading out his hands. "Now you want to know about the before times? Very well, I will try to explain. The analogy of the train could also be substituted by a waterway, a movement, from one place to the next. In this world, you experience time as a flow, a *direction* based on succeeding temporal instances inexorably linked with space and affected by velocity. Before creation, the experience of time was not as a river, but rather, an *ocean*. There was the experience of movement, of order and progression, but instead of a flow there was a *tide*, a tide pulled by love."

"Time pulled by … *love*? Seriously?"

"You know, the oldest civilization still existent on Earth is the Aborigine peoples of Australia. It was they who first understood the concept of a friend, a mate, and a kinsman. The Warlpiri in the north-central region call this person a *bungi*. To this day they say, 'How ya doing bungi?' This idea of relational connectedness, of bungi, is the fabric of reality. Where I come from, instead of space-time, there is bungi-time."

"I'm sorry, *bungi-time*?"

"Yes. In this physical reality, space and time are joined together, but before the beginning of space-time, before the spark of the physical universe, there existed—and still exists—a secret place, a reality where time and the interconnectedness of conscious beings are forever linked. The sequential state of kin-friend relationships, bungi, determines the passage of time. This realm consists of three elements: God the Father, God the Son, and God the Spirit. Past, present, and future event distinctions are solely based on our bungi relationship to each other. To explain this realm, I must use some imperfect, tensed language. We, being God, have 'always been' in perfect cohesion, perfect bungi. There has been no past relationship event with the three persons of God, no beginning, no initiation, only an objective reality. And with no beginning, there is no flow, no direction to time. There is no present per se, because the present presupposes a past, and no future, a concept which presupposes a past and present. In essence, this realm is *timeless* in that there has been no past, present, or future relationship instances. There is no flow of time, only the tide, which moves and comes again. Why? Because there has been no past, present, or future relationship *events* in our union as God that could demarcate these realities. God is that God is. And so, the dimension of bungi-time is timeless because there exists no succession of relationship temporalities. God is One, thus, God is timeless. The unity of God holds bungi-time in place, in effect, creating a time-*less* existence. There is no *space* to this realm, nor is there any matter. You cannot go there, you can only … *exist* there. In bungi-time, what is has always been and will always be, because of the immutable nature of God. It is both and, a kind of … *timeless* time. Why?"

"Because God is One," I answer, although the answer makes no sense to me.

"I have come to bring this physical dimension into our bungi-time reality, our secret place. Where the river meets the ocean, ALL will be One: God, Humanity, and Creation in perfect bungi. Distinct yes, but one. The unity of Creator and Creation begins in space-time but will extend into bungi-time. Humans have a name for this place. They call it *Eternity, Elysium, Valhalla, Heaven, Nirvana, Zion, Paradise … Shangri- La*. With God unified to physical creation in space-time and holding all relationships together, we can now bring ALL with us into tidal bungi- time … forever."

I scratch my head. "Eh, you're talking about a realm, a dimension in which the passage of time is based on the status of a relationship, and if that relationship has never changed, then there has been no passage of time?"

"Is it so hard to imagine time moving but not passing? The passage of time is affected by entities, by gravity, no? The very definition of time presupposes some kind of sequential experience of events. In this current, physical reality these are events based in space. What if, in another world, the sequence is based on *relationship*? And what if there is only one relationship? What if that relationship, that interconnectedness, has always existed and never changed? In such a reality, the flow of time would, in effect, spread out, and cease to flow. The quantum realm is my nod to the secret place of bungi-time. The new world I am creating will be a reconciliation of all creatures, and times, and worlds, and realities. Reconciled space-time will be integrated into bungi-time, it will be reconciled with God first, thus creating a seamless continuation of the tidal bungi-time dynamic, with its own unique temporal phenomena. You see, other events can occur within the tide *movement* of bungi-time, but only relationship events cause a *passage* of time, the flow from one to the other. And the spiritual world? It will be one with the physical world, a perfect reality, pure and redeemed and complete, a marriage of the tensed and tenseless realities within the confines of a forever present. Bungi-time has been imprinted on the hearts of humans. They sense its reality most in the face of death. Yes, death is the window into bungi-time because in death you sense most the passage of time. In me, indeed, in God, humanity will no longer be trapped in space-time. Past, present, future: these will be obsolete terms. No longer will humans experience time *passing*. Time passed is time lost, no? Ethan, you were made for bungi-time. I have come to break the hourglass of space-time. The days of sand pebbles trickling away are soon coming to an end. I will spread the sand on the sea of bungi-time. The tide will form beaches out of those minutes and seconds and hours. Together, we will walk once again and leave footprints in the sand of time."

"Oh," I say softly. "I see." Except I don't see, of course. I see death, yes. I understand death all too well. A memory of Vivian flickers in my brain and I resist the urge to tear up. Bungi-time sounds so absurd, illogical even. How can time not flow? It was incomprehensible.

"Now, a more interesting question is why I didn't make this perfect existence in the first place. Why wait billions of years in the darkness of space-time? Why the process? Ask me that."

"OK, good point. Let's see, Genesis, right?"

A finger points to the sky and Denim Guy quotes, *"And God looked upon all that he had made and saw that it was GOOD.* Not great, not perfect. Just … good."

It was an interesting thought. I mean, cells decay. Stars wink out. There is a ton of wasted space in the universe. There is no permanence to life.

"From a human point of view," I begin to say, then pause and change course. "Well, I admit, the universe isn't how a human would make it. We would make it so nothing dies, so it isn't dark and cold, and hostile. We humans like perfection and ease."

"You have spoken true, Ethan." Denim Guy stands up and stretches his back. "Humanity values the straightest line to perfection. But perfection can just be another word for *ignorance*. If everything was and always had been perfect, there would also be very little knowledge. *Good* is better than *perfect*. And do you know what is better than something being good?"

I shrug my shoulders.

"Something that is REDEEMED. To be redeemed, to have fallen and raised again, that, my friend, is true perfection. That is why I am here."

"To redeem humanity?"

Denim Guy peeks out of the lean-to tent flap door and stares at the sky. "Not just humanity, but all of creation. Space, time, gravity, quantum entanglement, these are primitive, rustic concepts, bordering on being illusory. The new world I am making will be much more … sophisticated."

BOOOOOM!

A concussive wave hits my chest. My ears ring. Dust kicks up on the floor. My heart pounds and I look around in fear.

"What … what was that?" I ask, wincing as I shake off the shock.

Denim Guy lends me a hand and raises me to my feet. "It's another incursion. Come, we must go. There are injured."

I grab my things and we rush out of the makeshift lean-to. Outside people are running in panic, screaming and shouting. A plume of smoke can be seen several blocks to the west. Denim Guy takes off down the alley to the main road. He turns left and I follow behind. Sirens blare in the distance. We run at a full sprint, dodging people and cars, and debris. By the time we reach the source of the smoke, I am gasping for breath. Denim Guy must be in some incredible shape because he's not even breathing hard. I barely have time to think about his condition though, as the scene at the entrance of the camp is one of horrific chaos. Dust and smoke fill the air, several people stumble around in shock, dust and blood covering their faces.

My stomach turns as we come upon a body lying in the street next to a burnt-out car. It's a boy in a green soccer jersey. Both his legs have been blown off in the explosion.

"Ethan? Ethan!" Denim Guy shouts at me over the screams and sirens. "Look at me, Ethan," he says, his voice becoming calm.

I know I'm in shock, but I turn my gaze away from the horror and look him in the eyes.

"No one will die here today, understand?" says Denim Guy with steady confidence. He nods to a place across the street. "You see that store over there? Fetch me some water."

"Uh, OK." I take a deep breath and try not to look at the boy's legs. Crossing the street, I see the windows of the store have been blown out. Inside, the shop owner is yelling at someone on the phone.

"Water? Do you have any water?" The shop owner doesn't acknowledge that I'm there. No time. I see a display fridge of bottled drinks. Leaving a wad of cash on the counter, I grab several bottles of water and run out the door. Machine gun fire erupts on the other side of the smoky haze. Bullets whiz by my head. I hit the ground and crawl to the burnt-out car.

Blood is everywhere on the pavement. My elbows and knees sink into chunks of flesh as I make my way across the street. I resist the urge to vomit. After what seems to be hours, I finally reach the destroyed car. Denim Guy is there on the other side of the vehicle. I just catch a glimpse of him helping someone to their feet. It's another boy with a green jersey. Was there a whole team here? Brothers perhaps? Denim Guy says something to the boy and points away down the street.

"Stand up, Ethan," he calls out to me. "Bring the water."

I do as commanded. Denim Guy opens a bottle and gives the boy a drink. Satisfied, the lad nods his head, then runs off to safety.

"Tourniquets," I say, choking through the smoke. "We need to apply tourniquets on the boy's legs."

"That is no longer needed," says Denim Guy.

"What?" I look down at the ground where the boy lay, except he isn't there. I see blood, lots of blood, but the injured boy is gone. "Did someone already come and take him?" I search around the area for emergency services. They still aren't here, but it's only been a few minutes.

Suddenly, it dawns on me. I turn back to the boy who just left, the boy with the green soccer jersey, the boy running on his own two legs. "No," I say to Denim Guy in disbelief. "It's impossible. Where is the boy who lost his legs? He was just here. Was that him? The boy who just ran off, did you …? How—" Words evade me, but it doesn't matter. My mind simply cannot compute what is happening. Denim Guy, he just calmly stares at me, as if to say, *"See, I am who I say I am."*

Shots ring out again. Bullets ping off the car. I take cover, but Denim Guy is unbothered. He stands there staring at me, the guy crouched next to the car, terrified out of my mind.

"Did you come here as a journalist looking for another human-interest story, Ethan Tellinger?" he asks. "Or did you come looking for something else?"

"What? I just wanted the story," I respond. "I don't know what you're talking about."

He kneels beside me with a knowing look on his face. "Maybe you came here looking for answers, not just a story. Well, what if I told you they are one and the same?"

Shouting erupts from down the street, followed by another loud boom. "Are we going to talk about this here?"

Denim Guy surveys the carnage. He shakes his head. "I have a proposal for you, Ethan Tellinger. Follow me for a year. Go where I go. Right down what you see. When the year is over, maybe then you will have your story … and your answers."

Another concussive blast is followed by dust and rock hitting my face. "Fine! Whatever. Let's just get out of here."

He takes my hand and pulls me up. "It's a deal then."

Not exactly my idea of a handshake deal, but that's what it felt like.

Just then a group of Palestinian men burst into the street armed to the teeth.

Denim Guy charges toward them. "Put down your weapons!" He yells in English first, then in Arabic. There is more talking and finger pointing between the man in blue and the group of militants, but eventually Denim Guy de-escalates, and they wander off one by one. Ambulances and fire trucks pour into the street. Emergency personnel fan out looking for the injured, but there aren't any to be found.

"Stay here," Denim Guy commands. "I will make sure they do not advance any further."

Without another word, he walks calmly into the dust, toward the Israeli military positions, straight into the firing line of their forces. Briefly, I see his silhouette through the smoke and flashing lights of weapons being discharged. In this moment of chaos I wonder what I have gotten myself into, and if this Denim Guy could really be the man he claims to be.

THREE
THE COMMUNITY OF SANT'EGIDIO

Rome, Italy
Wednesday July 21st, 2035

LEONARDO DA VINCI INTERNATIONAL AIRPORT in Rome is bustling as usual. I'm waiting at Terminal 3, looking for a glimpse of Denim Guy, aka Jesus of Nazareth. We exchanged email addresses in Jenin with instructions that he would contact me with the time and place of our next meeting. For three weeks there was silence, then, a few days ago, I get a message to meet him here. I still can't get over the idea of Jesus having email.

In the time since I left Jenin, my mind had begun to rationalize what I experienced there. It was all in my head, right? The mind-reading, the boy who grew his legs back, maybe there was something in the water. Maybe I was just caught up in the moment and didn't understand what was happening.

Back home in St. Louis, reality hit home. Most of my time was spent at Barnes Jewish Hospital, where the days were filled with waiting and tests, and more waiting. I replied to Denim Guy and told him I could meet for a few days, but then needed to get back home. So here I am, in Rome, with no idea what is going to happen.

A familiar Middle Eastern man in light blue appears in the corridor. He's talking with a few people, a woman in a hijab, a man in a business suit, a few teenagers. They exchange goodbyes and hugs. Whatever or whomever this guy is, he certainly has a way with people. Denim Guy is probably the most approachable person I have ever met. It occurs to me now that he has the ability to make you think you have always known him. I gather my bags and wave him down.

My hand extends out to greet him. "Long time no see."

Denim Guy ignores the hand and gives me a bear hug. "It's good to see you, Ethan."

The hug startles me at first, but I go with it. "Did you know those people?"

He shakes his head. "I just met them on the plane." "Yeah, about that, I'm surprised you flew here." Denim Guy shrugs. "How else would I get here?"

"Oh, well, couldn't you have just teleported or something?" I say jokingly. Denim Guy doesn't catch my sarcasm.

"I could, but I'd rather fly coach. It's a great place to meet people."

His directness stuns me, and I remember I need to get used to the weird things he says. "Right, of course, why didn't I think of that." Jesus flying coach opens a whole new batch of questions. Where did he get money? For that matter, how did he get a passport?

The questions must wait. Denim Guy takes my bag and starts walking. "You don't have to do that—"

He waves me off. "It's my pleasure, Ethan. You must be jet-lagged from the flight, and I don't have any bags."

I offer him my thanks and we head off to find transportation. Outside the terminal, Denim Guy hails a cab. He gives directions to the cab driver in Italian. Then we hop in and start rumbling down the road towards ... somewhere.

"So," I say, trying to make small talk. "What have you been up to in the last month?" Denim Guy buckles his seatbelt. "I've been in Madagascar, spending time with the churches and the Malagasy people. Have you been to Madagascar?"

"Never been."

"It's a beautiful country, with even more beautiful people." He points his finger out the window and says something to the cab driver. The cab driver nods his head, and a conversation takes off. My Italian is non-existent, but judging by the tone of his voice, it seems like Denim Guy is peppering the cab driver with questions about his life and work, and family. This is how it goes, I have come to notice. Denim Guy has an interest in everyone, especially everyday folk, the people you don't see as you pass them by, minding your own business. In fact, now that I think about it, *people* are the one thing Denim Guy seems most interested in.

A pause in the convo gives me the opening I need to ask my most pressing question. "Where are we going?"

"To the Vatican. We are going to see one of my followers."

While I'm left to wonder who this *follower* could be, Denim Guy and the cab driver pick up their conversation. By the time we arrive at St. Peter's Square, they are like long-lost friends.

The cab stops just beyond the Square on a street named the Via Porta Angelica. There is another exchange of hugs and a kiss on each cheek with the cab driver, who drives away, his face beaming.

On the sidewalk, we are immediately approached by a beggar, a young man wearing nothing but a sheet and a scarf wrapped around his head.

"A few dollars please?" the man says, walking right into my personal space.

I am suddenly stricken with panic. From experience, I know I should not give this person money. There is a whole ecosystem of beggary in Rome and there is no way of knowing who really needs money, or whether they are an actor, or maybe even both. But supposedly I'm standing next to Jesus, you know, the guy who preached the Sermon on the Mount? What do I do?

The beggar removes the wrap around his head to reveal a hideous wound on his scalp. It looks like he has some kind of leprosy.

"Please, a few dollars sir?" he repeats with his hand held out. Oh, come on.

Denim Guy looks at me. "What do you think, Ethan? Should we give him some money?"

It occurs to me that this is my personal Kobayashi Maru, so I choose my head over my heart. "I'm sorry," I say to the man, avoiding eye contact. "No money."

"Well, there you have your answer." Denim Guy pulls up the handle on my bag and starts walking, the wheels rattling down the cobbled sidewalk.

"Fucking Americans!" I hear muttered behind my back as we leave. Denim Guy turns to me. "Don't worry about him."

I nod my head like I'm not bothered, but I'm upset, and more than a little pissed off.

"Did you see his head?" I ask. "Yeah."

"I suppose he asked me because I'm American ..." "Yup."

He pats me on the back. "Just trust me here, don't let it bother you."

Well, too late. "Did I do the right thing?"

Denim Guy is focused up ahead, to where we're going.

"You'll see."

"Did he really need the money?"

My companion/bag-carrier stops on the sidewalk and looks at me. "Do YOU need money?"

I roll my eyes. "Well, yeah, I mean, I have bills, I need to eat ..." "So, maybe you are asking the wrong question. Never mind that now. C'mon, it's about to start. While in Madagascar I got on the internet and bought us some tickets." Denim Guy reaches into his pocket and pulls out two small pieces of paper.

"Tickets to what?"

He hands me one of the tickets. "A Papal Audience."

Naturally, I'm thinking this is a personal meeting with the Pope, but as we enter St. Peter's Square, I see thousands of chairs set up, and I realize this is one of the scheduled weekly appearances of the Pope for the general public. The ticket now makes sense, but I still haven't accepted the idea of Jesus using the internet. I shake my head at the absurdity of it all and remind myself this man is probably not *literally* Jesus.

We go through security, leaving my bag at the checkpoint, then make our way through the crowd and take a seat toward the back. Thousands of people file in, many of them already singing hymns. Out of curiosity, I allow myself to entertain the thought that they could be singing about the man sitting next to me. I turn to look at him out of the corner of my eye. Denim Guy is just sitting there, calmly looking around at the people.

Murmurs spread throughout the crowd. A small figure in white appears on the stage about two hundred feet away from us. It's the Pope.

The service begins and over the next thirty minutes, there is a homily, hymns, and a few remarks to the crowd, and a prayer. During the time of prayer, Denim Guy closes his eyes, but his lips don't move. He sings the hymns with the crowd in Italian. In the times of prayer, his head is cocked to one side as if listening. It was all very normal, save for the fact these worshippers might be worshiping my traveling companion. For his sake, he doesn't seem to find any of it uncomfortable or odd.

At length, the Pope dismisses the crowd and Denim Guy gets up from his seat. He moves to the front, and I follow. Patiently he winds his way through the throngs of people toward the barrier where the Pope is shaking hands and kissing babies. I know at some point after this we are supposed to be meeting one of Denim Guy's followers, I just hope it's soon because jet lag has me running on fumes.

The barrier is lined with faithful adherents, but we find an opening and wait for the Pope to reach us. The anticipation building, I stand behind Denim Guy and get out my phone to capture the moment.

Within ten minutes the Pope is there. He smiles at Denim Guy, shakes his hand. I snap a picture, then he moves on. Denim Guy doesn't move. He stays at the barrier. More people press in, desperately trying to touch the leader of the Catholic faith. I start to worry someone might get injured.

"Maybe we should move," I suggest to Denim Guy. "Just wait." He responds.

About fifteen feet away the Pope stops progressing down the line. He turns to look back in the direction of Denim Guy. Scanning the crowd he moves back to our position. Finally, the Pope settles his gaze on Denim Guy, his face a mix of shock, and joy. He motions to a security guard and member of the papal household to remove the barrier and allow Denim Guy to pass. There is some back and forth, with more stern commands from the Pope. Eventually, the security detail gives in. Denim Guy is helped over the barrier. He stands in front of the Pope, as cool and calm as if he were standing in front of me. What happens next takes everyone by surprise.

Without hesitation, the Pope drops to his knees and kisses Denim Guy's shoes. The crowd gasps at the scandalous sight. The cardinals who are a part of the Pope's entourage are horrified. The bodyguards are confused. Suspecting the Pope—an elderly man—might be having a medical emergency, they move in to assist.

Denim Guy holds up a hand. "Va tutto bene! Per favore, va tutto bene. Non c'è bisogno di allarmarsi."

The security guards freeze. Unsure, they look to the cardinals for direction, who offer none.

Slowly, Denim Guy kneels to cup the face of the Pope, which is wet with tears.

"It's you," the Pope says in wonder. "Mio Signore, Mio Salvatore, sei tu. It's you."

Denim Guy nods and smiles. And now he is crying too. They embrace, the Pope's head resting on the other man's chest. The crowd of onlookers begins to applaud, completely unaware of what's really going on. Embarrassed, I quickly dry my cheeks. I have to remain impartial, but I have to admit it was a moving scene. Who on earth was this guy? Am I being duped? Suckered into believing what I want to be true? What am I missing here? These thoughts skitter across my brain until it finally dawns on me that we have found Denim Guy's follower, the mystery person we are supposed to be meeting.

Both men speak to each other for several minutes, but I can't quite make out what is being said. I look around and see everyone doing the same thing I'm doing, recording the whole event on their phone and broadcasting it live on the internet for the whole world to see.

The cardinals slowly move in and help the two men to their feet. The Pope, still overcome with emotion, tries to gather himself. He is saying something else now. He points to a building over by the Basilica and forms his hands into a prayer motion. Denim Guy replies and points to me.

Uh oh.

"Sì, Sì naturalmente." I hear the Pope say. He motions to the guards. "Lascialo passare."

I put away my phone, and the security detail lifts me over the barrier. In a completely surreal moment, I now find myself standing between Jesus and the Pope ... no, no, no, it's Denim Guy, Ethan. Get it together. Denim Guy and the Pope. Just a couple of guys having a chat on a Wednesday morning.

Denim Guy introduces me to the Pope. I bow, because, well, because I'm not sure what else to do. "The Pope has kindly offered us lunch in the Papal residence," Denim Guy says to me. "There are other dignitaries there, and the other cardinals which he would like me to meet. But I have something else in mind." He turns to the Pope. "What if, instead, we went to the Community of Sant'Egidio and ate lunch with the Roma? I would like to meet them. What do you say? Would you serve the poor with me?"

The Pope's face lights up in revelation. "Yes, yes of course," he says, dabbing his eyes. "It would be an honor."

The next hour is a flurry of activity. Changing the Pope's plans at a moment's notice is not exactly easy. It was a logistical nightmare, but eventually, around noon, the details had been sorted out, and we found ourselves in a motorcade on our way to the Community of Sant'Egidio, a humanitarian organization run by the Church.

"Have you heard of the Community, Ethan Tellinger?" Denim Guy sits next to me in the back seat of a car, the third in a long convoy of black vehicles. He is practically giddy with the excitement.

"Not until today."

"They are legendary in heaven. The work they are doing, it is incredible, and it is almost entirely run by laypeople. They help the elderly, migrants, the disabled, prisoners, children."

This is great, but I'm still stuck on the Pope. "I suppose if you had told me the person we were meeting was the Pope I wouldn't have believed you."

"He's been a follower of mine since he was a boy, so I knew he'd be up for a change of plans."

Within minutes we arrive at the piazza where the Community is located inside a church. Attendants coordinate with the volunteers who have already prepared plastic bags of "meals on the road" for the homeless, which are then loaded into the motorcade. Before we leave, Denim Guy and the Pope take time to meet individually with the staff of the Community and thank them for their work. We are then shuttled to the Roma Termini, the main transportation hub of Rome where many of the Roma gather. Word has spread of our little outing, and we are greeted by a handful of media and cameras, along with the public. Denim Guy joins the Pope and I follow behind. All of us have our hands full of plastic bags of food. Together we are led by a Community staff member to the location of the Roma.

There is a group near the opposite entrance on the north side. They consist of women and children and men. To my dismay, I recognize one of the men. It's the man in the sheet who was asking for money! Denim Guy turns and grins at me. Good grief, you've got to be kidding me. This is my worst nightmare.

The Roma are spooked by the huge entourage and almost leave, but the Community worker convinces them to stay. Denim Guy and the Pope speak to them in Italian. They begin to hand out bags of food. There are no tables, so we sit on the dirty floor. Unwashed children dig into the bread and meat and fruit without hesitation. They run around all of us, laughing and playing, completely oblivious to the fact they are eating lunch before all the world with Jesus and the Pope on the disgusting tile floor of a subway station. I envy them. The Roma adults are more wary. They eat the food quietly, sometimes shielding their eyes from the flashing lights of the media, who are broadcasting our meal to the world. I can only imagine what is being said on CNN right now. Denim Guy starts to make some conversation, and over time the adults become more relaxed. They explain their life, their hardships, their families. The young man in the sheet mechanically eats his food. We try to avoid eye contact with each other.

For his part, the Pope appears to be in heaven. I don't think I have ever seen a man as happy as the Pope eating lunch with Jesus and beggars on a filthy floor.

A child plops down on Denim Guy's lap and the man in blue doesn't miss a beat. He tickles the youngster who then lets out an uncontrollable giggle.

It was a fleeting instant, but for a second everyone seems so relaxed I almost forget the surreal nature of the moment, and I simply enjoy a meal with friends. There was nothing else to do, nowhere to go. We just ate and talked and laughed, then ate some more. Minutes stretch to hours. By the end of the meal, Denim Guy and the Pope are like family to the Roma, that is, except for the young man in a sheet. He still seems upset by our presence, or maybe it is MY presence that bothers him. Denim Guy seems to notice too, so he takes the young man aside and speaks to him privately. I can't hear what is being said, but the young man is shaking his head, apparently refusing to listen to what Denim Guy is saying. Suddenly, the peace of the meal is shockingly interrupted.

"Fuck you!" the young man shouts at Denim Guy, his voice echoing throughout the station. "Fuck you to hell! You don't know me." The young man throws his food on the ground and runs off.

Concerned, the Pope stands up and goes to Denim Guy who doesn't seem particularly surprised, certainly not offended.

"It's OK," he says reassuringly to the Pope. Denim Guy comes back and sits next to me. "The jury is still out on that one, but I think he'll come around."

"Really?" I ask with as much incredulity as I can muster. "Yeah, I don't know. He seems angry, and dangerous."

Denim Guy stuffs some of the leftover food into a bag. "You were right not to give him money."

"I was? That's a relief."

"He was faking his injury. It was just some makeup and prosthetics. He DID need your money like everyone needs money to live, but what he needed even more was respect. Dignity. That's what we gave these people here. It wasn't just food. It was dignity."

I help him clean up the napkins and paper plates. "Will the Community help these people?"

Denim Guy looks around at them. "I doubt the Roma would accept their help, but the Community will try. It's what they do. They are the experts. The Roma, most of them are honest hard-working people. Even those who panhandle. Kneeling on stone pavement eight hours a day begging is hard work, let me tell you. Yes, some of them are criminals, pickpockets, actors, silent beggars using piety and the gospels to induce tourists to give. They do what they can to survive. This world has not been kind to them. I am making a world where people like this don't have to just survive, but a world where they can really live as I intended. And the other people, the dishonest ones, the fakers, and deceivers, I can't help but love them too. Like that young man. He hates all the world as he hates himself. But there is hope for him yet. No one is hopeless, Ethan Tellinger."

The Roma disperse without so much as a thank you, but Denim Guy and the Pope don't seem to notice. Their gratitude is communicated in their own way I suppose. Blessings and prayers are offered to the Roma as they leave. The children want to stay. They cling to Denim Guy, refusing to go. He kisses them on the forehead and says a prayer for each one. One by one their parent wrangles them up and they disappear into the fading golden light of late afternoon.

Denim Guy shields his eyes from the sun and quietly watches them depart.

FOUR
FLIGHT 8172 DEPARTING

Somewhere over the Atlantic Ocean Friday, July 23rd, 2035

CRAMMED INTO THE MIDDLE seat of coach, Denim Guy and I pick at our in-flight dinner. Well, I pick at the tasteless food. Denim Guy gobbles it up while chatting up the person sitting next to him, a transgender man in his 30s. To my surprise, Denim Guy has agreed to accompany me back to the States. What he wants to do there or where he wants to go is still unknown.

For the last two hours, a child has been crying in the row in front of us. With seven hours left on our flight to New York, I rub my temples and take a deep breath. A flight attendant comes by and takes our food.

"Flight attendants," Denim Guy says to me. "They are saints, no?" He hands his tray to the steward and then gets up to speak to the mother in front of us with the crying baby. After a brief exchange, the mom hands the child to Denim Guy. Almost immediately the baby stops crying. He cradles the infant in his arms and rocks her back and forth. Exhausted, she falls asleep.

The TV screen in front of us is showing CNN in non-stop coverage of our encounter with the Pope, who is now doing interviews proclaiming Denim Guy to be the Christ, the Son of God.

"So it begins," says my companion, as if he planned this whole thing from the start.

Overnight, the world order had been turned upside down. Social media is blowing up with everyone's take on the man sitting next to me. Denim Guy is now the most talked about trending person on earth.

I see my moment of opportunity and hit record on my phone, having ditched my old analog recorder a few weeks ago. "Can I ask you something?"

Denim Guy moves the baby to his shoulder and pats her back. "Sure."

"How did you get money and a passport?"

He shushes the baby first, then rubs her back some more. "One of the benefits of being the all-knowing, all-powerful Creator of the universe is that you know where to find buried treasure."

"Come on, seriously?"

There's a twinkle in his eye. "Don't get me wrong. I'm always working, always helping people, fixing things, but I'd rather not charge a fee for those services. I don't need money, other than to buy a ticket. So, I monetize what people have lost or left behind throughout the centuries. Whatever excess there is I simply give away to the poor."

"And the passport?"

Denim Guy reaches into his back pocket and hands it to me. It's an Israeli passport. I open it up. The name: Yeshua bar Yosef. Country of Birth: Israel. Date of Birth: 09/17/02.

I flip through the pages. I see a stamp from Madagascar, India, Jordan, Yemen, Sudan. "Looks normal to me. It says here you're only 33 years old."

"Well, kind of. Technically, I put my birthdate as 09/17/2* as in, September 17th of 2 B.C., but the computer requires two digits for the year, so the government worker who processed my application put down 02, as in 2002 *AD*, thinking I just forgot to add the leading zero. I figured it was pointless to correct, so I let it go."

I can't help but laugh. "Wow. Um, OK."

Denim Guy takes the passport and places it back in his pocket.

"In Rome you mentioned heaven. Does that mean hell is real also?"

"Hell is a spiritual reality, a place, the ONLY place completely devoid of our presence."

"OUR presence?"

"The presence of God, what has come to be known imprecisely as the Trinity. The Father, The Son, and the Holy Spirit."

"Oh, right." I jot down some notes on a napkin so I don't forget that sometimes he speaks in plural pronouns. "And this Hell, it's a fiery place of eternal torture?"

"There is a myriad of historical orthodox views of hell. Some view it as a metaphor, some a kind of purgatory, others think of it as a temporary place of refinement or a universal reconciliation, still others see it as annihilation. More recently, the view that hell is a conscious place of eternal torment has become popular. All these views have been held by my faithful followers for hundreds or thousands of years. Some are more correct than others. Whatever your interpretation, hell is not a place of *torture* per se. More like … *torment*. There's a difference. A headache can be torment. A crying baby on a ten-hour flight can be torment. 120-degree heat in a desert without water can be torment. Non-stop bitterness can be torment. Would we call those things torture? Maybe, maybe not. Probably not, though. The point is, hell is a miserable place for miserable beings—most of them fallen angels—who don't want to be around me. This is the crowning feature of hell. It's a place devoid of my presence. That isn't to lighten its horror. You don't want to go to a place devoid of my presence, believe me."

I decide to add a follow-up. "Are there any other misconceptions about hell?"

Denim Guy takes a sip of his coffee. "The biggest misconception about hell is that all the souls who are there want to escape. I once told a parable about a rich man in hell who was thirsty. Outside of hell, he sees Abraham perfectly in peace. He asks Abraham to cross the chasm and bring him water. Now, isn't it interesting that the rich man thinks Abraham can bring him water in hell? Where did he get that idea? If he thinks Abraham can reach him, then why doesn't he ask to be rescued? Everybody in hell hates it there, but not everyone wants to leave if leaving means they must live in eternity with me. That would require an admission of wrongdoing, but hell is filled with the self-righteous, and the fact that they are suffering—in their minds, *unjustly* suffering—only hardens their heart even more. If you read the scriptures, I never really force anyone to do anything, but I also don't spare people the consequences of their actions. If someone wants to live a sinful lifestyle, I let them do it. I don't interfere. The only exception is if that lifestyle violates the liberty or personal autonomy of another person. Then, I will step in. It is why we established human systems of accountability to deal with murder, theft, and other crimes.

"I also intervene when there are unjust systems established to oppress the poor and weak. The poor and the poor in spirit are my special charge, the apple of my eye. Whoever offends or abuses the poor and weak will be punished, they will be punished eternally unless they repent and offer recompense to the ones they victimized."

"Eh, OK. Got it." I make a mental note to revisit this idea of recompense.

We hit some turbulence. The plane shakes and drops. A few people gasp from the sudden change in altitude. The seatbelt light comes on. People begin to stir and wake up. I see Denim Guy lift a finger, a single finger from his left hand, the hand holding the baby. Immediately the air smooths out and the shaking stops.

The coincidence makes me wonder … could it be possible? Hm, nope, nope, nope, don't go there Ethan.

I pretend like nothing happened. "So, um, how exactly does someone make it to heaven?"

"Through me," says Denim Guy. "And only me. I am the Door to eternal life."

"That's it then? Just, blind faith?" His eyebrows lift. "Oh, if only it were that simple for people. The fact is *faith* is a loaded term. Belief is one part, yes, but faith also means you must trust, and trust enough to follow unto death. The deeper you progress in your faith, the more the 'Gate' to eternal life gets smaller, which means you have to *make* yourself small to enter, remember? This is easier for the poor in spirit, but much more difficult for the proud, the learned, the wealthy, the privileged, the able. Someone could believe I am the Son of God, that isn't so hard actually. I mean, even the devil and his demons believe I am the Son of God. So clearly that is not enough. Another person might trust me to save them but not believe I am whom I say I am or want to follow me where I go. They just want to be saved for ulterior motives. So that is not enough either. A person must believe, trust, and follow … and keep following, even unto death. Some don't make it that far, but I am the Good Shepherd, I go beyond human abilities to hold on to what is mine. Even then, someone can wander away if they are determined to, if they indulge a *hell* state of mind rooted in bitterness. They cannot be stolen from me, but they can leave of their own accord."

"Ah, now we're getting somewhere." I sit up in my seat. "So, you are not a determinist then? Humanity *does* have free will?"

Denim Guy pats me on the leg. "I have *determined* it to be so."

"Clever, very clever."

He gives me a thumbs up.

"I guess that means you are not, what they call a Calvinist? Or maybe it's that you are a limited Calvinist? How does that work?"

The baby passes some gas and wiggles around. Denim Guy pats her back. "Theology is a servant, not a master. No one's theology is perfect, but generally, the poor and weak have better theology than the theologians. Whether it is the Pentecostals, the Reformed, Orthodox, Catholic, Calvinist, Molinist, Arminian, etc., all see in a mirror dimly, as Paul says, but when they meet me face to face, they will see clearly. Just as you are doing now, Ethan. The question is always whether someone can accept what I say as truth, or will they choose to hold on to their opinions. Can someone admit they are wrong? If they can, then a miracle has occurred. Repentance and grace are the super miracles. Raising the dead is easy. Casting out demons? Give me a break. But softening a hard heart? Redeeming what is lost? There is nothing more miraculous than these phenomena."

"OK, but back to …"

"Calvinists are partly right; I have pre-ordained everything to happen. It's the *scope* that they get wrong. What does *everything* entail? Arminians are also correct in that atonement is for everyone. EVERYONE. I want everyone to be saved, anyone can be saved, but in the world that I have *pre-ordained* to exist, not EVERYONE will want to be saved, not everyone will want to be around me. I would be a weak God if I could not accommodate another free will other than my own. It doesn't reveal anything about my glory to pick and choose who is chosen for glory and who is chosen for damnation. That's a human way of thinking, like a spoiled child who must get his way by exerting his will OVER everyone else. But there is great power in weakness too. There is great power in holding back, in allowing not everything to turn out exactly the way you want. There is power in being meek and gentle. Poverty of Spirit, this is the great super-power. With it, humans can do anything. There is even greater power in choosing to suffer when you didn't have to suffer. Why? Because this is true love. And so, I have chosen a people to be my people, and human beings can choose if they want to be part of my people. They are not left alone to choose. I help them, the Spirit helps them. In the end, no one has an excuse. We do everything we can to see that each person is saved."

"But what about the remote peoples who never heard of you? The lost tribes in the Amazon, are they basically ... screwed?"

"Certainly not! I judge people based on what they know and what they are capable of knowing. That is justice. There are people in heaven who never heard my name on earth, but they followed me nonetheless because the Spirit witnessed to them, and they heard because they are made in my image. I tell you the truth, many indigenous tribes in the West worshipped me long before the Europeans."

"So, what, in the end, God is ... *good*?"

Denim Guy checks the baby's diaper. "All the time."

I hit pause on my phone. Mom is fast asleep in front of us, but from the smell now hitting me in the face, it's clear that baby needs a diaper change. Denim Guy leaves his seat and grabs the diaper bag from the overhead bin.

"I'll be right back," he whispers to me.

A few minutes later he returns. Baby is still asleep. Denim Guy climbs over the person to his left and settles back into his seat.

"Now then, where were we?"

I click record on my phone. "How about I change the subject to bioethics?"

"OK."

"What are your views on abortion?"

Denim Guy switches to a cradle position with the baby. "My heart breaks for every abortion, and there are over a hundred thousand abortions every day, give or take. These tragedies are coupled with all the others that occur every second. Have you had your heart broken?"

The idea of heartbreak causes my eyes to flicker to my phone, where I am expecting a notification to appear at any moment.

"I think that's a *yes*," Denim Guy replies to his question while glancing at my phone. "Well, my heart breaks millions of times a day, every day. It breaks for the women who feel they must get an abortion. I have a lot of love and grace for them. In fact, I have a lot of empathy and grace for people who are in any kind of ethical dilemma that forces them to make a tough decision. We must admit reality, the reality that sometimes there are no good choices. This is love. Alternatively, I have much less grace for societies that do not value children and families, societies that do not empower women, or even attempt to hold fathers accountable. These are unjust societies. Look, if you want less abortion—as I do! —then you would empower women instead of taking their rights away and violating their physical autonomy."

"I have to admit," I interject for a moment. "I'm kind of surprised by your response. Your followers, Christians, they are mainly focused on changing laws so that abortion is illegal."

"Why would you want abortion outlawed if the effect could be that the law *increases* the loss of life, and does what you do not want to do? How is that pro-life? You better be sure what effect your actions will have. This is not like murder or theft or any other crime. Outlawing these crimes does not increase their occurrence like it could with abortion. In the case of the latter, you've made it so that more women are going to die. I want to save lives, not endanger them. Sometimes that means Christians need to back off, have less power, not more power. In this way, we should advocate for the unborn, not through force, but through love. Not every problem can be solved with a stroke of a pen. We must deal with the world as it is, not as we want it to be. I don't like pitting one life against another. I would never do that. All throughout history women have been abused and undervalued, but did you know, most of my followers are women? It has always been so. And the growth of my church has been primarily through and by women."

"Are you a feminist?"

Denim Guy pauses a moment, his head tilted to one side. "Depends. The term *egalitarian* probably fits better, but words are never perfect, are they?"

"So ... women in leadership roles, women as pastors?"

"Oh yes, women are wonderful teachers and pastors and leaders. Look, it was a woman who wrote the book of Hebrews, so, all Christian men—whether they like it or not—have been taught by a woman and sat under her biblical and spiritual teaching."

My phone alerts me that the battery is low. "Can I ask one more question with a follow-up?"

I get a thumbs-up response.

"What are your views on sexual ethics?"

Denim Guy gives me a mischievous smile. "Sexuality. It's a bit antiquated, no?"

The question throws me for a loop. "Um, *antiquated*? How do you mean?"

"Sexuality is part of the old world passing away. The new world will have no such thing."

"Well, a lot of people are going to be disappointed," I remark.

Denim Guy is certainly committed to the new world/old world theme. Whatever it is, it sounds, dare I say it, boring?

"Think of it this way," Denim Guy continues. "The age of sexuality is like the age of the horse and buggy. The new age will bring electric vehicles, making that old horse and buggy obsolete. Which would you prefer? The car with air conditioning, heated seats, Bluetooth, and that can go 75 miles per hour, or the horse and buggy where you go ten miles an hour, freeze to death while having a beast passing gas in your face?"

"Obviously, I'll take the Prius. But a world with both options is kind of nice."

"Imagine you live in the 1800s and someone describes to you the concept of an automobile. It sounds strange and terrifying. A machine speeding down the road with all these buttons and contraptions? It's overwhelming. Why? Because all you know is that horse and buggy. This is the corollary to humans and sex. Sex is all you know … for now. But that is changing. A new thing is coming that will make sex antediluvian, such that you will wonder how you ever lived with sexuality at all. What is coming will be better, much better, but trying to convince you now is useless, like explaining a smartphone to a caveman."

I clear my throat. "Even so, what about the here and now?"

"It's a level playing field. The question for homosexuals and bisexuals is the same as heterosexuals, and those who identify as pansexual, asexual, omnisexual, and every other kind of sexual orientation."

"Which is …?"

"Will they deny themselves and follow me? The implications of this question pose a problem for every human, regardless of what gender or sexuality they identify with."

Well, OK then. "I can see why not everyone wants to be around you," I say dryly. "No offense."

"None taken."

I shift position in my seat and turn toward him. "It's just that, well, in the modern world this is, you know … an intolerant view, and to be honest, it sounds kind of hopeless."

"Not if someone picks up their cross and follows me, whatever that cross might be. This is the Life. I would never punish or fault someone for having a same-sex attraction. I am not here to change someone's desires, not really. I am here to give them a NEW desire. Unhitch that horse. Let him go to the green fields. There is a shiny new electric car on the way, and it's specifically designed with you in mind. A new creation will have new desires, desires that may come into conflict with the desires of the old creation. It is this conflict, this *tension*, that is a mark of my followers, but spiritual superposition takes time to bear fruit, decades, perhaps even a lifetime, and usually never completely. That's OK. You can't force it. I don't force people to abide in me and my way. People can live as they see fit if they choose. This evil conversion therapy going on is a brutal sin that slams shut the door of the Kingdom that should always be open."

Denim Guy lifts an eyebrow and gives me a side-eye. "Open, but *small*. In truth, I will tell you this: the age of sexuality is coming to an end. The whole idea of sex is passing away for everyone, it's becoming out of date with each day I am here in this world.

"Until then, have faith in me. I have grace for people who need to figure things out. The greatest amount of sexual sin in the world is *hetero*-sexual in nature. Will straight men stop harassing and exploiting women? Sexual abuse and the concealment thereof for the sake of my Kingdom is perhaps the greatest sexual sin. Silencing victims with NDAs is a hideous kind of wickedness that is truly detestable to me. Can I tell you something? It can be harder for heterosexual men to pick up their cross than it is for those who are gay. Want to know why?" he whispers, leaning in close.

"It is because they are the most self-righteous. It's hard for someone self-righteous to become small. And what happens is, they create a stumbling block for others who might follow me. And my followers? They are most effective when they live to unbelievers as *fellow* sinners, not righteous people. Because that's what they are … sinners. They are best when they preach *up* to people, not down to them. My true followers, they have a leanness of soul, a sense of restraint and spiritual modesty. Spiritual modesty is great faith, Ethan. It is an emptying of yourself and your preferences and opinions. In my Kingdom, small faith is big faith."

"Right, the, um, the mustard seed …"

"Correct! I search the earth for small faith. I look for weakness to complement my strength. I hear little prayers, earnestly given. For me, I am attracted to neediness. I am drawn to the lost and forgotten. The question for me—as I told you before—is whether someone's weakness will be weak enough to accept me. It is not righteousness that connects me to a person, it is *sin*, and I have an undying love for sinners. I want to wash their feet. I want to sanctify them. But can someone accept this from me? It is possible to have a false pride in Christ. Many people would like to see me powerful, on a throne, robed in glory and hurling thunderbolts, not robed in a kitchen apron, or changing dirty diapers."

"All right, expound on that. You've laid a lot out here. In the simplest terms, what is the nature of your true followers?"

He takes a beat and exhales a long breath. "The truest sign of being my follower is not that someone is clean, but that someone is being *cleansed*. It is not enough for someone to be clean. This is not enough. They must be cleansed. This is the essence of Christian spiritual formation, not in being pure, but in all things, being purified. They are my people, not just because they do or believe something, but because I *wash* them. The issue is not in their cleanliness but in their cleansing. It is not in their works, but in their washing. I once told the disciples, 'If I do not wash you, you have no share with me.' Notice, I did not say 'If you are not *clean* you have no share with me.' No! I said, 'If I do not WASH you, you have no share with me.' Many want to be clean, very few want to be cleansed! Many want to be pure, very few want to be purified. Many want to be spotless, very few want to be sanctified. Sheep never want to be sheared, but they need it. I told you before, the Gate is small. Well, now you know why."

At this point I need clarification: "But do you realize that many people wouldn't find this to be fair? Many—"

Denim Guy nods his head. "It is not necessarily the existence of objective moral precepts and obligations that people find unfair, Ethan Tellinger. Even nihilists believe in a truth they say is absolute: *'Life is meaningless,'* they say. Nor is it the idea that someone might impose their morals on someone else. A crazy person might believe he has the right to murder someone, but society imposes its values on him and prevents him from doing what he believes he has a right to do. Sure, this is an easy, extreme example. But what about tolerance? In a fallen world, a free society will accommodate different points of view. This democratic value to *agree to disagree* is the most ideal for a country and it is imposed on everyone for the benefit of society. So, what is really happening in human hearts? What do people really find unfair? It is the concept of *self-justification*. The idea that someone, anyone, can *truly* earn. I agree with them. But think about this: what is it about earning that people are working for it while at the same time finding it unjust? The dissonance is readily apparent. This is the witness of the Holy Spirit that each person possesses. Deep in their souls, people know they are not enough, no matter how much they deny it, no matter how hard they try, no matter how much good they do. They know it is folly. They know because they are created in my image. When someone thinks they have earned salvation, they are faced with the feeling it doesn't ring true. Something is still not right. They must decide if they will listen to this voice, or if they will reject it because no one can earn anything. Why? Well, perhaps they were privileged to earn. Maybe they had access to more knowledge and resources to earn something that someone else did not have. Or perhaps they failed in some other area. Maybe they won the genetic lottery. Just to *seek* to earn a status is to introduce a motive of self-preservation that taints everything else and robs the person of truly earning. Humanity longs for justification, but they can't find it anywhere. They also long for grace and mercy, two concepts that necessarily presuppose the existence of moral precepts.

"So, what is fair? I tell you what is fair: Save for the little children, ALL have failed. All have fallen short. Rich and poor, healthy, and unhealthy, across the entirety of the cultural and political spectrum. No one has earned anything. All have sinned, but no one is all bad and no one is all good. Atheists can be good moral people. Someone can be a sinner and a victim at the same time. I told you once before, a sinner is a human. That is true with one exception: ME. And so, it is by me and through me that someone can finally find their justification, and thus, their peace. The more a person thinks they are self-justified, the further they are from me. Many of these types claim to be my followers, but I am closer to sinners than I am to the righteous because the righteous don't need me. It is the person who knows that they have not earned anything that is finally justified. The righteous find the wicked to be abhorrent and evil, but both are blind. The former more so than the latter."

"Not sure I follow." I tap the pen on my chin in thought. "But OK. Seems like you're getting back to this cross-carrying idea."

"Correct," he replies.

Mom wakes up in front of us. She thanks Denim Guy for holding the baby, which he returns to her still sound asleep.

"Salvation is a cross-carrying event," he continues. "It is both inclusive and exclusive, available to all who can walk the narrow way. To follow me you must bear your cross, problem is, a lot of people have trouble finding their cross, or if they find it, they don't want to carry it. For sinners and victims and the disadvantaged, their cross is easier to find, in many cases it is already on their shoulders! For the privileged, it is much harder. They don't have a cross when they come to me, so they must find it and follow me. This is a tough ask: to go from being burden-free to freely choosing to be burdened. You can see why it is so hard for them."

I check my phone for that as-yet incoming alert. "Yeah, I guess so." I feel my blood pressure rising as the seconds tick toward that one notification. His words bring to mind a story from the gospels. "Like the rich young ruler. Whatever happened to that guy?"

"I could tell you," he says. "But sometimes, knowing the outcome of a story robs the effect it could have."

The little plane on my TV screen shows us moving past the midway point over the Atlantic.

I stifle a yawn. My phone dings. There it is. I let out a sigh of relief.

It's OK. All is well. "I have a lot more questions, but that's enough for now. My brain needs a break. I'm going to get some shut-eye. I imagine you're pretty tired as well."

Denim Guy shakes his head. "Not really. I don't get tired."

Huh. Of course. "OK, Forever Man, whatever you say. You still gotta tell me what that name is all about."

"I thought you would have figured it out by now."

I shift around in my chair, trying to get comfortable. "Nope."

"Hey, don't forget, Ethan, you still need to pop the BIG question.

The one you've been dying to ask me. I haven't forgotten."

Always back to this. THE question. Denim Guy just wasn't going to let it go. I ignore him and drift off to sleep.

FIVE
SAVING PASTOR ABRAHAM

South Chicago, IL. Saturday, July 24th, 2035

O'HARE IS PACKED WITH travelers, par for the course on a late-afternoon/early-evening Saturday. We were supposed to fly into St. Louis from New York, but our flight was diverted due to weather. As far as airports go, it wasn't the most popular, but it had a special place in my heart. O'Hare International was the departure destination for my first flight out of the country when I was seventeen. I still get a sense of wonder and excitement when I arrive here.

Together we navigate the crowds and eventually make it to my rental car. We hop in and I can't help but notice that my companion buckles his seatbelt.

"Do you really need to do that?" I ask, referring to the belt buckling. "If you are God then you are indestructible."

"It's the law, isn't it?" Fair enough.

We get on 294 and head south. Not fifteen minutes in, Denim Guy instructs me to take the next exit. I'd rather not stop—there is still five hours of driving left to go—but I indulge my fellow passenger because I'm always curious what he is going to do next. Without using any kind of map, Denim Guy directs me to the parking lot of a McDonald's. I figure we are here to meet someone, but when we go in Denim Guy orders food and sits down at a booth.

I am completely lost as to what is happening, so I barely touch my milkshake. Denim Guy notices my consternation.

"Sometimes," he says over a mouthful of food. "You just need a quarter pounder with cheese, you know?"

We both share a laugh. If you would have told me a few minutes ago that Jesus of Nazareth loves McDonald's I would have committed you to an institution. I have come to learn to expect the unexpected with Denim Guy. Despite whom he is or whom he claimed to be, he was always down to earth. After our meal, we head back to the counter. Denim Guy greets each of the workers. To my irritation, one of them decides to share their whole life story. I check my phone for alerts. Denim Guy listens intently, completely enraptured. The same thing happens with another worker. And another. And another. Suddenly I notice the whole atmosphere of the restaurant has changed. The staff is now laughing and joking with Denim Guy, their spirits lifted. The most time is spent with a quiet middle-aged man in the back assembling burgers. Denim Guy puts his arm around his shoulder. The man becomes overwhelmed with emotion. Apparently, he has just been released from his second stint in prison.

"I can't believe this is my life," the man says through tears.

Never in a million years would it have occurred to me to speak to these people and hear their stories. I would have gone through the drive-thru and barely acknowledged they existed. But Denim Guy is hopelessly drawn to service workers, the *invisible people* he calls them. A few of the staff seemed to have seen the news about my companion, they share the news stories of the Pope's encounter with their colleagues which garners a whole new round of excitement. A bona fide celebrity is in their midst, and it's the Lord of the Universe. Well, by the time we leave it has been nearly three hours since we arrived. Hugs are exchanged. The staff comes out to the parking lot and waves goodbye.

Back in the car, Denim Guy clutches his chest in pain. "Heartburn?" I ask, half-joking.

"I'm OK," he says. "Let's get going."

I get back on 294 South. It's now almost 9 pm. Denim Guy rubs his chest, a worried expression on his face. A few minutes pass. I put on my blinker to get onto 55 South.

"No!" Denim Guy shouts. "Not that way." "Uh, St. Louis is south."

"We have to go north." Denim Guy winces in pain. "He needs my help. I can feel his anguish. Quickly now, there isn't much time."

"He? He who?"

No answer. Alarmed, I do as I'm told and get on 55 North, driving back into Chicago. The further into the city we get, the more Denim Guy seems like he is in pain. A few miles in he points to an exit, which I take, and we drive into the south side of Chicago. After a series of twists and turns Denim Guy has directed us into Englewood.

"Turn left here," he says.

I turn left on a street and we're heading back north. I see a decrepit church on the right, juxtaposed by a newer church campus on the left. The tiny church on the right has been left in disrepair with weeds growing around the front, chipped paint, and graffiti tagged on the walls. A faded sign says Church of the Redeemer in bold lettering.

"The building on the right," says Denim Guy. "That's the one."

The bumper of the car scrapes the pavement as I pull into the lot and park. Denim Guy jumps out of the car. He runs into the building through the front double doors and I'm right behind him.

Inside, the pews on each side of the sanctuary are empty. The faded green carpet is loose and torn in some places. Brick walls are crumbling, but the stained-glass windows still retain their beauty. A cross is stationed on the wall behind the stage, which has only a wooden pulpit on its platform.

Denim Guy stops halfway down the middle aisle. To my shock and horror, an older black man in a suit and white clergy collar kneels on the floor in front of the pulpit. He's holding a gun to his head.

"I'm sorry Lord," I hear the minister say. "I can't do it no more. I gave you fifty years, fifty years of blood and tears. Never took a dime. Wear the same old clothes every day. Now it's all gone. They're gone. They're all gone. I'm so tired. Please forgive me. I'm just a stupid,

stupid man. I just can't ... Where did you go? Where are you? Answer me! Where are you!?"

"I'm here," says Denim Guy.

Surprised, the minister turns and points the gun at Denim Guy. He clambers to his feet and wipes his face with his other hand. A look of suspicious confusion is on his face as he inches closer to us.

"J-Jesus?"

"It's all right, Abraham." Very slowly, Denim Guy puts a hand on the minister's arm, lowering the gun. "I'm here. I've always been here, at Church of the Redeemer, right here with you."

"My God. It IS you. Jesus Lord. My Jesus." Abraham drops the gun. He covers his mouth and begins to weep. Staggering backward, he collapses to the floor, his eyes fixed on Denim Guy in wonder.

Denim Guy sits beside Abraham and holds the man's head to his chest. I breathe a sigh of relief and decide I need to sit too.

"I'm so sorry, Lord," Abraham says. "I failed. I despaired, lost faith. Some pastor I am, huh? Don't even know how I could ask forgiveness."

"Oh, my dear Abraham." Denim Guy wipes his face. "There is nothing to forgive. You haven't lost faith. All these years you followed me faithfully. You followed me all the way to Gethsemane."

"But Lord ..." Abraham stands up. "What kind of shepherd loses all the sheep? I done lost everyone. I lost 'em to the hood, I lost 'em to the big church across the way, I lost 'em to drugs, to guns, to temptation, to poverty. When I first started as pastor here, I had such high hopes to restore this community. Now look. Fifty years later, nothing's changed! Folks still scared, still suffering. The police are powerless. You know, in the beginning, I was glad when the big church came here. I thought we could work together. They had all this money and resources. Together, I really thought we could raise people up here, give back to the community, maybe finally do what I always dreamed of. Oh, the big church, they gave a little, just enough to post pictures on their social media, but that ain't enough. I tried to tell 'em, Lord, but they never returned my messages. I called, tried to set up meetings. They always had a bunch of programs going on. That's why I didn't even begrudge the people leaving our church for theirs. I didn't blame them. Look at this place. Who would stay here? We got nothing. Nothing! Besides, they ain't my sheep, they're yours. Who am I to hold on to what ain't mine? But now, those who left are going back to their old ways, back to hatred, back to thieving and gambling and fighting. Decades I worked, it's all for nothing, man."

Abraham rips open his shirt to reveal a thin body marked with scars. "I've been shot, stabbed, robbed countless times, defrauded, beaten like a dog, doused in kerosene, nearly set on fire in the middle of the street. One night, the drug dealers, they broke into my house and tied me up naked with barbed wire. I didn't hate 'em, not even then. I prayed for their forgiveness. Well, they just laughed and spit on me. Took two days before one of our elders found me, almost dead. My whole body is covered in these scars."

"Folks here, they're so poor, I never could take a full salary. So I worked the second shift at the factory, survived on food stamps and second-hand clothes. Then the factory closed. My wife, well, she finally had enough. She left a few years back. I don't blame her. What kind of man can't provide for his family? Huh. I even lost my sons to the gangs. Still, I felt called here. I loved this community so much. Just never could make it right. Then a few weeks ago, the few that were left, we was having a church picnic in the park. A car came by. I knew who it was. Well, they roll up, guns blazing. Seconds later, they're all dead. My whole congregation, all ten of 'em killed. What I want to know is why couldn't I have been the one to get shot. Why couldn't it have been me, Lord? I just don't understand it. I prayed and prayed and prayed."

Abraham looks up at Denim Guy. "Well, Lord, what can you say to an old failure like me, a pastor to an empty room?"

Denim Guy dries his eyes with his sleeve. He holds out a hand to Abraham, who takes it, and lifts him to his feet.

"Only one thing I can say." Denim Guy places a hand on the minister's shoulder and whispers. "Well done, good and faithful servant."

Abraham buries his face in Denim Guy's shoulders. "Ethan, could you give us a moment?"

I step out, deeply moved by Pastor Abraham's story. Maybe

Denim Guy really was whom he said he was. How could all of this be a coincidence? If someone like Abraham believed, who am I to say he is wrong? What is stopping me from believing too? In the back of my mind, I know what could convince me, but I have to ask him THE question. This reminds me to check my phone for alerts. There's a new message. Oh, no. I must get home.

SIX
IN THE WORDS OF KAGAWA

Interstate 55, Illinois Sunday July 25th, 2035

GIVEN HOW LATE IT was, we decide to stay overnight in Chicago. The next morning we're back on the road. For the first hour Denim Guy sits in the passenger seat next to me, his eyes closed. Not surprising. He didn't sleep at all last night, but I knew he was going to need sleep eventually. Suddenly his eyes open.

"There you are," I say. "And here I thought you would never need sleep."

"Oh, I wasn't sleeping. I was listening."

"Listening? Listening to what?"

"Prayers." Denim Guy looks out the window at the endless rows of corn passing by.

"Oh, right. You know, I must admit, you do have good listening skills."

"Listening is not a *skill,* Ethan Tellinger. If it were, more people would be good it at. Want to know a secret? Listening is a *discipline.* It requires continually keeping your mouth closed, and your mind attentive." Denim Guy stretches his neck. "Traits like listening, leadership, management, and administration, most people do not understand these things. A wise Catholic priest once said, 'Be a manger, not a manager.' Take Pastor Abraham for example. You tell me, was he a good leader?"

Usually, I might just say yes, but Denim Guy has got me thinking. "In some ways. But it depends. Based on the Western kind of capitalistic, entrepreneurial idea of leadership he was not a good leader because, on that standard, well, he wasn't very successful."

"You have spoken correctly about Western values. In all actuality, Pastor Abraham was a great leader and an even greater follower. The American view of leadership is fatally flawed."

"Is that right?"

"In the West, they think leaders are born or made. Neither is true. There is no such thing as leadership *traits* or leadership *characteristics*. There are lots of influential, charismatic personalities who are terrible leaders. Why is this? Leadership is something that must be learned but cannot be taught. One problem with the Church here in the US is that everyone wants to be a servant leader, but no one wants to be a servant. Me? I'd rather just be a servant, even so, first and foremost the number one task of a leader is to *anticipate crisis*. Whether it be a pastor, a CEO, a president, or community leader. Leaders must prepare for calamity. Leadership is a foul-weather job, you see."

"Hm, that's interesting." I click on the cruise control and relax my legs. "Nowadays everyone thinks the number one priority for a leader is to have a vision. That's what I've always been told, at least."

Denim Guy shakes his head. "Never rate a person by the fact they have stirring visions or good ideas. Beware of all inward impressions. They are rooted in pride. And pride is another word for dishonesty. People tend to glorify age, youth, personality, or giftedness. But what old age knows is considerably less than what it ought to know. Older people have loved their idols longer than young people, and therefore have become more like those idols. Love of a youthful spirit is also an idol. A whole lot of stupidity and pain has been caused in the Church for the sake of someone's vision. Big vision is the product of ambition and is almost always the precursor to spiritual abuse. Ever has it been so."

"Why is that?" I ask.

"No matter their intentions, people will end up loving their vision more than they love people. They will do anything to achieve this vision, even at the expense of everyone else. And so, they become wolves, not leaders. They prey on the sheep and spit out their bones. In many churches, they prioritize the able and the gifted. The weak and needy are left behind. But these weak and ungifted people, they are sacred in my sight. The church needs them more than anyone else. If you want to know if a church is healthy, look at how they treat those who can do nothing for them. You'll get your answer soon enough. No church is perfect. I can tolerate many things, but abuse and ambition will incur my wrath."

"Woah," I say in surprise. I've never heard him use a word like *wrath*. "That's heavy."

"You said it brother. The penalty for sin is not determined by the amount or severity of the sin but by the magnitude of the one who has been sinned against. Take note."

"Yeah, I'll ... do that."

Windmills appear in the corn fields on this stretch of I-55. Denim Guy sits up in his chair and studies them.

"My church is like those windmills," he says. "The wind is the Spirit, causing the church to move and produce power, the fruit of the Spirit."

Denim Guy sits back in his chair and looks straight ahead. "Pastor Abraham produces a great deal of fruit. Maybe not in the eyes of the world. But in my eyes, he has done very well. He has been a servant and a sufferer, like me. He held to the truth even when they tortured him. I have followers like this all over the world, but you will never hear about them. They don't seek attention. They don't want glory. They have no big vision, no grand plans. They only want to love and do my will."

"Too bad they aren't more well-known," I say wistfully. "It's always the big mega-church pastors that are famous ... or infamous."

I wait for a reaction from Denim Guy, but he gives none.

"About the big mega-churches," I continue. "What do you think about those?"

"Churches are bigger than ever now," he says. "But overall, fewer people are going to church. Remember what I told you in Jenin, my followers are few and far between, but you can always find them anywhere. I have followers in big churches and small churches, churches that are healthy, and churches that need healing. Size, in and of itself, is not wrong, but it's harder for big churches to be what I desire."

"Really?" I ask in befuddlement. "From where I stand it looks like they are doing pretty well, they are even successful you might say."

"Ironic, no?" Denim Guy folds his arms and tilts his head to the side. "My church is, in truth, the city of the poor. The big ones, the mega-churches, they have a lot of people. They also have a lot of bills, a lot of egos, a lot of baggage, a lot of pressure, a lot of competition, a lot of politics, and a lot of reputation to uphold. It's not impossible for them to hit the mark, but it's more difficult. Their consciousness of their reputation and influence is what gets them in the end. They let their left hand know what their right hand is doing. Power becomes concentrated on one person because the church doesn't want a shepherd, it wants a CEO with business leadership, not spiritual leadership. From there it is academic. Sheep get left behind because it now becomes untenable to leave the 99 for the one that got away. The 99 are more needed to support the weight of the group. But if a pastor can't leave the 99 for the one, then the church is too big and should divide into smaller churches. And so, in big churches, it happens that they love the 99 more than the one, because to go after the one, you must leave the 99 untended. This is a poor business model. Why would you risk losing everyone for just ... someone? Big churches are risk-averse. They must accommodate, and the temptation to get high on their own supply is too much to resist because they are human. They become a *seeing* church, a church that only sees its buildings and numbers and baptisms. And so, the ministries start spinning their wheels, they work harder not smarter. The illusion of productivity is created on social media, but no one is transformed. Discipleship becomes an assembly line to create more engaged contributors, which is to say that discipleship is non-existent. A false sense of community is created. The promise of comfort and riches brings people back, with the prerequisite of tithing. The whole system becomes transactional. My name is invoked ad nauseum, but I am largely absent, save for the hearts and minds of the children and a few earnest followers." He looks over at me. "Am I answering your question, Ethan Tellinger?"

"Yeah, I think I get the idea."

"I'm speaking in generalities and the tendencies of humanity. It's important not to pigeonhole denominations or specific churches. For the most part, people don't intend their church to become what I just described. It just happens that way because people are human, and humans are ruined by success far more than they are by failure. In many ways, success is a curse, a big shiny, attractive curse. I tell you truthfully, those big churches will never be as successful as the failures of Pastor Abraham and the Church of the Redeemer in Englewood."

"I see. Well, not really. I'm going to have to think about that."
"Hey, you know what I am really like?" Denim Guy sits up in his chair, suddenly very excited.

I shrug.

"I would never seek to assert myself. I would never try to be the center of attention. I am a listener, a helper. I am happy to be the assistant. My passion is to do what no one else wants to do, in the places where no one else wants to go. I don't glory in myself and my power, even though I could. It just isn't me. I would never dominate or show off. I'd rather work in the nursery, or clean up after people, or be the support person, the clerk in the office. Let someone else take the glory."

"Well, you are good with babies," I remark. "But honestly, I mean, supposedly you created everything. You are God, right? The King of Kings. It's OK to get some credit."

"I don't seek it. I don't seek equality with anyone, I seek to be *lower* than everyone. A servant of all. That is who I am in my nature. I have a meek and gentle personality. I lower myself, and the Father glorifies me. It has always been that way."

"Kind of the opposite from some of your followers." I say this with a touch of disdain and feel I must add a rejoinder, "Again, no offense intended."

Denim Guy affirms with a nod, so I move on.

"Something else I've noticed. Why don't you spend more time with your church? I mean, I realize we were just at a church, but overall, I figured you would want to spend more time in churches with your people. You seem to gravitate toward other places."

"I am always with my church, even now, in this car, and to the end of all time. I am with them, and they are with me at all moments. They abide in me, and I abide in them, even as I am with you now."

"Sounds very … mystic." I make a mental note of the fact that at times Denim Guy can sound more modern, and at other times more like the Jesus of the Bible. At the present moment, he is sounding like the guy in the gospels.

"Oh?" Denim Guy replies thoughtfully. "It's definitely spiritual. But only I know who are the sheep and who are the goats. The sheep know me. The goats use me, but they don't know me, and I don't know them. Their goal is power and independence, but my goal is loving kindness. My church can never grow through force or political power. Civic pluralism, and classical liberalism, these are the ways to the most just society in a fallen world. Now, to the onlooker, it may seem like there is an ebb and flow to the influence of Christianity and the Church in the world, but it is a mistake to think of these things from a worldly decline/renewal framework of thinking. What may seem to be decline could actually be renewal. What may seem to be revival might actually be decline. I build my church; I am the Head of the body. Only the Head can see and know the true health of the body."

"The sheep and the goats analogy is helpful. Sheep follow and graze—"

"And goats are more exploratory," Denim Guy cuts in. "They like to browse, and investigate, which leads them to be found in many interesting places far away from me. They are more independent and curious. Most of all, they are stubborn. They are forever nibbling on different things. And so, shepherds separate the sheep and the goats because the goats can injure the sheep. The sheep are simple followers. The goats are independent, those who want to be the greatest—"

"Greatest Of All Time!" I interject. "G.O.A.T."

Denim Guy throws up his hands. "Well, there you have it. Sheep require more care. They need shearing. Goats want to do their own thing. There are mainly differences in behavior. American evangelicals in practice believe the one thing that matters is correct belief, and that following me is a secondary afterthought. Which is why they are great at evangelism and poor at discipleship. In reality, they are also bad at evangelism too. What they are truly good at is proselytization, which is much easier than making disciples. Many people think they are a sheep, but they are actually a goat. I am the Good Shepherd and I know who is who."

"Does it bother you that many of your followers can't agree on what is right?"

"Such as?"

"Well …" I decide to go with the first thing that comes to mind, a topic we briefly touched on over the Atlantic. "Women in leadership."

"Women have been in leadership in my church since the beginning. They have been pastors, apostles, deacons, church planters. In many ways, they are more naturally suited for leadership than men. Men are prone to pride and dominance, which leads them to not listen to the truth if it comes from someone they despise. As for myself, I would sit under the preaching of any man, woman, child, or donkey who would speak to me the truth. What matters is the truth, not artificially constructed gender roles. I often speak to people through the voices of those they despise. Do you look down on women? Then I will send a woman to preach to you. Why? Because pride plugs peoples' ears. Pride must be addressed before listening and transformation can begin. To your larger question of disagreement, what I am building is unity, not uniformity. My followers cannot follow me if they cannot learn to love those they disagree with. To follow me means to forgive like me.

You cannot forgive like me unless you have been wronged like I have been wronged. In the end, you will know my followers by their fruit. Do they love? Do they forgive? Do they give up their rights for the sake of others? Are they meek and lowly of heart? Do they speak the truth in grace and kindness? You will never know them by what they believe. Even the demons believe. You will know them by their fruits. Does their work involve spiritual, physical, and social liberation? They will show you their faith by their works. They will not just tell you about me, they will embody me in this world. A living sacrifice. It is the only way."

A thought pops into my head. "Doesn't sound very practical."

"It is most definitely NOT practical. The Beatitudes are not practical. Loving your enemy, or even your neighbor, is not practical. If it were practical, then people wouldn't need me to do it. Practicality is the idea of making something doable. But my ways are not doable, not in human terms. My strength is needed, and my strength needs weakness to work through to be glorified. People throughout the centuries have tried to make my teachings practical, so people can do the work independently of me, like the goats we spoke of earlier. But it never works. Humans need me to be *like* me. They must have poverty of spirit, leanness of soul. I am attracted to neediness.

"What are some great examples of your true followers?"

"I assume you mean someone well known, so I'll give you the name of someone famous who truly resembled me. Toyohiko Kagawa."

The name vaguely rings a bell. "Kagawa. The ... 20th-century socialist and reformer?"

"I don't think he would call himself a socialist, but yes. He was also a pacifist. As a young man, he moved into the slums of Kobe and lived with the poor in a hut."

"Ah. Like how I found you in Jenin."

"Exactly. He once preached on a street corner until he became ill and almost died. When his fellow students at the seminary were faced with expulsion, he took their punishment and left the seminary so they could stay and attain their Bible degree. He was often without clothes because he would give them away to the poor. One time he had to wear women's clothing because that's all he had. Kagawa would give anyone anything they asked of him. Why? He loved the poor and wretched for my sake, and he suffered for it. He was and is a man transformed by my love, the truest friend. He was ridiculed by the Church and other Christians. They thought him crazy, devoid of any profound thoughts. A fool. Many want to be wise and great in my name, but I seek people who are willing to become fools for me. There aren't many of those."

At this time, it occurs to me that I have forgotten to record our conversation. Kicking myself for the oversight and blaming it on jet lag, I fish my phone out of my pocket. I'm stunned to see my phone has been recording the whole time.

"How ...?"

"Everything OK?" Denim Guy asks.

"Uh, yeah. I guess so. That's so weird." Suspicious, I glance over at my traveling companion. He glances at me, a somewhat amused expression on his face. Convinced it's just a coincidence, I decide to move on.

"You mentioned prayer before, so I was wondering...do you pray?"

"Yes, I pray for my followers, I pray for the world."

"And what is the significance of the Lord's prayer? Were you telling people how to pray or what to pray?"

He takes a deep breath. "Prayer is a manifestation of *poverty*, not power. There is not great power in prayer, there is great poverty. Many of my teachings can only be understood through poverty. I love what Kagawa once said ... *If a Christian does not love the poor, then they are not a Christian. My religion is not elegant, it is a sewage-gatherer. My followers are refuse collectors, cleaning up and redeeming the filth. It takes more power to redeem than it does to create. If you have plenty of food, then you will never understand the meaning of the Lord's prayer. The way of the cross is the way of the economic lowly, the way of children, and the oppressed. It is the way of love, yes, but love is consistent with danger. Christianity is a simple religion, understood by babes. Children understand prayer more than adults. Grown-ups tend to pray long-form and philosophically focused. But prayer is intuitive and instinctive. The prayers of Jesus in the Bible are very short. Christ's longest prayer in John 27 was only five minutes, and yet he spent a lot of time in prayer. The point in prayer is not to seek what God hides, but to be faithful in what he reveals."*

"Would you mind if we did some rapid-fire questions?" I ask.

Denim Guy shrugs. "Of course."

"What are your views on death? And for the matter, what was it like to die?"

"For my followers, death is sweet. It is the culmination of the cross-bearing life and the last act of repentance. All of discipleship is the dying to self and coming alive to Christ. What was it like to die? For me, it was like victory."

"Victory, OK." I go to the next question. "How much time should someone spend in Bible study?"

"A lot of time. But it's a mistake to think that someone cannot understand the Bible without minutely studying it every day. Sinners can understand the Bible more than the righteous, certainly more than theologians and scholars. So, when it comes to Bible study, eat what you can. Many have become my followers by studying the parts they could understand. A greater question is on what the purpose of the Bible is. The Bible, the Word, it is given to reveal my inner consciousness. Many Christians miss this. Students and learned people who have never attempted to bear the consequences of the failures of others simply cannot grasp this fact. Taking the sorrows of the world as their own is a mystery to them, but it is my way. My followers must bear the consequences of others, this is my solidarity-responsibility consciousness that Kagawa loved, filling up the measure of what is lacking in the suffering of Christ. This is Christianity, my religion. In the academies they love ideas, but ideas alone are valueless. Deeds must express them. Religious life is not extraordinary, it is simply to reveal God in our daily life, in the problem of poverty. This is also Kagawa."

"And what is the secret of God, what is ..." I pause to formulate the wording. "If you could communicate one thing about God, what would it be?"

"The omnipotent God suffers to save even the least of his children. That is all. This reality is the crowning feature of Christianity and the greatest revelation of God to mankind. To be my follower, you must prepare yourself for suffering because I am a sufferer. We suffer when others suffer. We suffer to save and redeem."

"Next question: Next week in Nashville there is a big leadership conference of the biggest protestant denomination in America. Any advice for them?"

"Generally, I am uncomfortable in religious conclaves."

"Really? Even if it is your own church? Your own people? Why is that?"

Denim Guy looks at me deadpanned. "It was a religious conclave of my own people that had me beaten and killed, Ethan."

"Oh, right. The uh …" My mind searches around but the name of the group eludes me.

"The Sanhedrin." "Right."

"Here's the thing," Denim Guy continues. "These meetings must happen, but people should be wary of them. They require wisdom and humility. Very often in these settings, that is when you get the hangers-on of authority, the takers, and the mischief-makers. Kagawa believed there were two types of Christianity: success Christianity, and failure Christianity. Denominations must choose, will they follow me even to failure and death, or will they choose the way of worldly success."

"OK, what are your views on work?"

"Work is good, I am always working, as I have said. But work is not the purpose of life. People are given life so that they may live."

"Sounds like a quote. Let me guess, Kagawa?"

Denim Guy gives me a wry grin. "What can I say? I'm on a roll."

"Next question: are you a pacifist?"

"Only the strongest can commit to non-violence. It is a power from the next world, a special calling only for some. In the Colosseum, my followers would pray for the forgiveness of the Romans as they were torn to pieces by lions or burned alive at the stake. They did not resist death and torture. They gladly died. And what happened? The hatred of the Romans melted away under such supernatural love. Pacifism is also the way of my kingdom, the way of eternity. One day, everyone will be a pacifist. At the same time, like Kagawa, I have a fondness for fights. Not because of the violence, or anger, and foul words, but because I like the idea of justice struggling for victory. Again ..."

"Kagawa's words, not yours. Got it." This was kind of an interesting non-answer, but I decide to move on. "Can someone have too much money?"

"Those who have been entrusted with money, and gifts, and abundance, have been entrusted with God's provision. But those who have been entrusted with poverty and affliction have been entrusted with God's strength. So, which is greater, God's strength or God's provision?"

"This next question is a bit open-ended. What is love?"

"Kagawa said it best ... *Christ is love. My nature impels one to love. This desire in me is greater and mightier than the desire in humans to sin. Love is the great reformer. You can always judge a society by how much it loves. Love is kind and meek. Love has very few words. The religion which seeks to exploit people will always use the greatest number of words. They will publish many books and plan many conferences. True love is gentle and fierce. It is unassuming, not self-aware, but confined to the needs of today, not tomorrow, and full of grace and mercy. Love is not the opposite of hate; love is the opposite of perfection. It absorbs imperfection, is content with imperfection because it knows this prevents self-satisfaction. A person filled with love will allow themselves to be carried about like a little child who does not even ask where they are being taken. Love will toil in the darkness without seeing the fruit of the labor. Love is content with daily bread. Love suffers long. Love takes what comes and does not run after what does not come. Love gives no heed to likes and dislikes. It is the purest when not stimulated by award. Love hates to be great but adores to become a little child. Love fits a person for physical death by the daily dying to self. Love is willing to be overruled. Love is not shocked at the great faults of others. It seeks nothing. Love is wary of intellectual gifts; it abides in simple faith.*

"Love dies daily and is born daily. Love knows it is better to be crucified with me, than it is to read about my sufferings. Love leads with action and allows words to come after."

"Very well," I briefly interject. "But perhaps in your own words, you could …"

"Love does not convince itself what a person is like. Love is content to not know everything. It sets aside opinions. Love does not hurl Bible verses at people. Love would rather make one disciple than 10,000 leaders. Love waits for those whose progress is slow. Love does not weigh and calculate. Love gives all and is not aware all has been given. Love keeps no record of rights, nor any record of wrongs. Love abhors false charity and ambition. True love takes no pride in being right, but it loves to be corrected. Love bears the consequences of others. Love knows it is more extraordinary that the poor are blessed than for the dead to be raised to life. Those who love others more than themselves are those who truly love themselves as God intended. So, you see, the self-absorbed don't love themselves too much, they love themselves too little! Complete love of self is loving others more than yourself. People are given an awareness of self, so they can lay that self aside in self-expenditure for the sake of another. This is God's love. If there is nothing to lay aside, nothing to deny, then there is no love, no virtue. When all is said and done, love pours ointment on the head of God."

SEVEN
PRISONERS OF CHRIST

Jacksonville Correctional Center Sunday, July 25th, 2035

"YOO DA FOREDA MON?" asks the sullen charging station clerk, speaking in a Jamaican patois. We have stopped in Springfield for twenty minutes to recharge the car battery. After perusing the aisles for snacks, I'm loaded with chips and candy. My phone is currently blowing up with messages. Evidently, word has spread around media circles that I am with Denim Guy. The interview and meeting requests from national media, world leaders, and NGOs are non-stop.

"Mia da Mon, Sistah," Denim Guy replies with a warm smile. "How lang hab yuh bin yah?"

"Sumweeeeh, lakka six months," she says, beginning to tear up. "Tings a suh bad eena jamrock, mi did hav tuh kuum yah fi safety. Mi arrived pan ah boat. Almost drowned mi did. Now mi a worry 'bout fi mi court date. Mi hope di judge will let mi tan."

Denim Guy takes her hand. "Everytin' gwinna be ai-ree, Sistah. Jus bi yuhself, yah? Tell dem unnu story. Yuh a neva alone. Mi be deh too. Duh yuh ave any fambily wid yuh?"

"Fi mi cousin a yah, buh mi madda an pupa a eena *jamrock*."

The conversation plays out like so many others. By the time we leave, Jaqweshia the clerk is hugging Denim Guy and kissing him on both cheeks.

"Puppa Jesus, Puppa Jesus," she says over and over. "Gloria Puppa Jesus."

I have no idea what this means so I look it up on my phone. No surprise, it is the Jamaican patois for Jesus Christ.

Denim Guy reassures her again that all will be well and that we had to leave, but that he was still with her and praying for her.

"Keep di faith," he says in parting. When we arrived at the station twenty minutes ago Jaqweshia was looking quite despondent, now it looks like she has just won the lottery.

Back in the car, we open the snacks and hit the road. I'm munching on Doritos. Denim Guy has a candy bar in one hand and a beef stick in the other. I'm just about to merge onto I-55 South when Denim Guy grabs the wheel.

"Stay on 72," he says over a mouthful of food.

"But St. Louis is that way," I say, pointing to the left.

"Jacksonville Correctional Center is West. I have arranged a special visit for us."

I'm confused. "Um, OK. And you were going to tell me this when?"

"Right now."

"Look, I need to get to St. Louis soon. And my phone is ringing off the hook from people all over the world who want to meet you. I'm talking about presidents, monarchs, the UN, the head of NBC, even Oprah. What should I tell these people?"

"Tell them they have to wait. I must go to Jacksonville Correctional Center."

"Whatever you say." I put the car into self-drive and begin replying to messages.

"One of my closest followers," Denim Guy continues. "His name is Siddhartha Patel, Sid for short. He has ministered there quietly at the prison for many years. I want you to meet him. There are also followers among the inmates that I must see. A group of them meets for a worship service every week. I love listening to them sing and play music. Worship from prison is the purest you'll find, my friend. And don't worry, you'll be in St. Louis by late afternoon."

Irritated at the change of plans and the fact I am now basically a personal assistant, I create a form response and let all the officials and producers know that Denim Guy is not doing interviews or meetings at the moment because he must go to a prison in Jacksonville, IL. I have absolutely no desire or interest to visit a prison, but I feel obligated to go. How do you say no to such a kind man?

"Not sure Oprah has ever been rejected before," I comment, then hit send. "But it just happened."

Forty-five minutes later guard towers and barbed wire fences come into view. I pull into the parking lot of Jacksonville Correctional Center. A short man in his 70s is there waiting for us. He has a grey mustache and a warm smile.

Denim Guy and Sid greet each other like long-lost father and son. I'm introduced to him. We shake hands.

"Imagine my surprise when I get a message from you-know-who," Sid says, nodding to Denim Guy. "I felt something in my spirit, and I just knew it was Him. Jesus." He gives Denim Guy a side hug and wipes his eyes. "That he would come here to be with me, with us, here in the prison. It's just, it's overwhelming."

"But I'm always here, Sid," says Denim Guy.

"I know, I know." He clasps his chest. "Come on, let's go inside. The boys are going to love seeing you, but there's a bit of security to go through first, then they will escort us through gen pop, to the annex where we meet."

We follow Sid to the prison entrance, which is a side door on the main administrative building. There is a metal detector to walk through, then our IDs are handed over and we fill out some forms. Our belongings, including phones, are placed in a secure locker.

Fifteen minutes later a guard is leading us through the yard to the annex. On the opposite of the open area, I see inmates lined up, waiting to enter the annex. Some of them wave to Sid. He waves back.

The annex is attached to the gym. Inside I see about ninety chairs set up. In the front, there is a wooden podium. Behind this, there are various musical instruments like a keyboard, guitars, amps, a drum kit.

A set of windowed double doors leads to the gym, where various inmates peak through in curiosity, then go back to playing basketball or lifting weights.

Sid and Denim Guy line up by the door and wait for the men to arrive. The guard sits behind a desk, and I lean against the wall not too far away. The door opens, a man in a blue inmate's uniform walks in holding a Bible. He hugs Sid. Denim Guy shakes his hand with a big smile and greeting. One by one they come in, each of them with dark blue pants and light blue button-up shirt. All of them are excited to be there and see Sid, who greets these imposing, tattooed men like they are his grandsons. Initially, they are taken aback by the presence of Denim Guy, but being the ultimate people-person that he is, it's not too long before the feeling in the room is that he is someone who belongs in a place like this.

For my part, the inmates glance at me with suspicion and curiosity. I try to melt into the wall. There are about ninety people in the room. A small percentage of the ten thousand that are housed in the minimum- security prison. We are given plastic chairs to sit in. The band takes their positions, and a group of the inmates stand together in the front as the choir.

The music starts. I clap along, but the songs are unfamiliar to me. Sid leans into my ear. "They aren't allowed music or sheet music, so they have to write their own songs."

In my thirty-nine years, I have been to many concerts. The skill and musicianship of these inmates at Jacksonville Correctional Center rivaled anything I had ever heard before. The fact that they wrote these catchy worship songs made it even more impressive.

Denim Guy enjoys it so much he begins to dance. The choir is singing a song about "King Jesus" and I wonder if they realize they could very well be singing about the guy standing next to me. After about forty minutes of songs and prayer, Sid steps up to the podium. "A few weeks ago, I got an email from a friend," he begins, gesturing to Denim Guy. "He said he wanted to come see you guys, and I was so happy. It was the greatest email I ever received and I'm never deleting it. Well, most of you met my friend when you walked in. He goes by many names. His reporter friend, Ethan, he calls him Denim Guy for the blue clothes he wears, just like all of you! For me, I've only known him by one name … Jesus. Jesus of Nazareth. Jesus the Christ."

The guard puts his phone down and sits up in his chair. A shocked murmur spreads through the crowd. The inmates look around at each other in confusion. Some of them shake their heads in disbelief.

"Hey Jesus!" someone shouts from the back. "Get me outta here, bro!" Laughter breaks out.

"Quiet down!" the guard yells. He calls for backup on the radio.

Just when I think things may be getting out of control, an inmate stands up who looks to be of Pacific Islander descent. He is very quiet and reserved, and almost seven feet tall! His brown arms are bulging with muscles and Samoan tattoos. He's one of the biggest and most intimidating men I've ever seen. His name is Macarius, but Sid informed me that everyone here just calls him Big Mac. He makes a move toward Denim Guy, then hesitates. The room goes silent.

The nervous guard gets up from his desk.

"It's all right Ryan," says Denim Guy to the guard with a hand up, his eyes fixed on the giant towering over him. "Come closer, Macarius." He motions for the enormous inmate to stand in front of him. "Do not be afraid. I want to see you."

The big man falls to his knees. "Jesus?" His deep voice rumbles. Tears well up in his eyes. "I … I can see you. When I first came here, I was just a prisoner of the state. Now I am a prisoner of Christ."

Additional guards enter the annex bearing riot gear.

Macarius looks around at everyone in the room. "Boys, I can see him! It's Jesus! He's here!" The gentle giant buries his face at Denim Guy's feet at begins to laugh, or possibly weep, which one I cannot tell. Maybe both.

"Hey ya'll," says the keyboard player into his microphone. "Big Mac is right. I see him too. It's Jesus!"

Denim Guy takes Big Mac's face in his hands. He stands up, and Macarius rises to his knees. Even with Macarius kneeling and Denim

Guy on his feet, the inmate's head comes up to Denim Guy's neck. Denim Guy takes that massive head and holds it to his chest. A look of complete peace is on Big Mac's face. Sid is on his knees, his hands over his mouth in a praying position.

The band and the choir come forward and gather around Denim Guy. "It really is him!" they say, touching his clothes and face. Soon, the whole room is gathered around, ninety prisoners all trying to touch Denim Guy.

Realizing the compromising position Denim Guy is in and fearful he could be attacked with a shiv, the guards move in to break it up. Once again, Denim Guy waves them off.

"They cannot hurt me," he says. Flabbergasted, the guards back off.

A chant starts up from the prisoners. "Je-sus! Je-sus! Je-sus!" Denim Guy shakes his head and laughs. He speaks to every inmate.

I chat with the guards and Sid for a little bit, but mostly, we all look on in marveled silence. A few prisoners are still skeptical. They challenge Denim Guy to an arm-wrestling match, convinced a skinny 135-pound man could never beat them. To my astonishment, Denim Guy complies. He sits down with each prisoner and patiently arm-wrestles each one. None of them can even budge Denim Guy's arm. The slight, 5'9"-ish Middle Eastern man beats every one of the muscled prisoners with a casual smile and not a drop of sweat. He even overpowers Big Mac. Now five of the prisoners are arm-wrestling Denim Guy at the same time and with the same result. The exhausted inmates shake their heads in disbelief.

It's decided that we take this to the gym. Things are getting serious. Forty-five-pound plates are added to the bench press bar, totaling just over five hundred pounds. Denim Guy lies down on the bench. He picks up the bar—which is bending considerably—for a moment his arms tremble, but then Denim Guy says, "Just joking," and does ten reps, again, without breaking a sweat.

"How is this even possible?" I say to Sid. "It's absolutely remarkable."

He laughs and slaps me on the shoulder. "Brother, you ain't seen nothing yet."

More weight is added. 750 pounds. Same result. Ten reps, no sweat. Big Macarius tries lifting the weight. Not even he can get it to budge.

Still, more weight is added. Now over 1,000 pounds. Pretty sure this would be a world record. Well, it's the same result, except this time Denim Guy does twenty reps, not ten. The whole gym is hooting and hollering in disbelief. To put the icing on the cake, Denim Guy stands up and effortlessly lifts the 1,000 pounds with one hand over his head.

The chants start up again. "Je-sus! Je-sus! Je-sus!"

Eventually, the feats of strength are completed, and things calm down. It's time for the inmates to return to their cells. Denim Guy takes Big Mac aside and speaks to him in private. An earnest discussion is happening. He speaks briefly with many more inmates and a few of the guards. I am always curious to know what is being said in these conversations, but I don't want to intrude. Maybe some things are best left in private.

One by one the prisoners file out, the same way they entered. It's mid to late afternoon. In the parking lot, Sid is on cloud nine.

"Remember," says Denim Guy to Sid. "I am with you always. Even when we leave here, I am still with you. Thank you so much for your faithful service." He looks back at the prison, past the barbed wire fence. "I tell you now, there's gold in them hills."

Sid admires the prison too. "Aye, there sure is."

We say our goodbyes. I unlock the car and open the door. Denim Guy doesn't move.

"Ethan Tellinger," he says. "This is where I must leave you for now."

I'm completely caught off guard. "Here? Oh, OK. Um, well, do you need money or …"

Denim Guy gives me a hug. "No, no. But thank you."

"Hey, what was that all about in there?" I ask. "I thought you didn't like to show off and draw attention to yourself?"

Denim Guy kicks a rock. "Well, I figured the cat was out of the bag, might as well remove any doubt for some of the others, and create a little camaraderie. They needed it. Those really are my people in there. Places like this prison. That's where you will find me. Not on Oprah, and I love Oprah."

"So, when will we meet again?"

He looks away for a moment. "Soon. I'll send you a note with the time and place."

"OK."

There is an awkward silence, and I realize Denim Guy is waiting to see if I ask him THE question. I think about all the things I've witnessed him do and say, including most recently, lifting 1,000 pounds over his head with one arm. None of it mattered. For whatever reason I couldn't bring myself to do it. I couldn't ask him what I wanted to ask him. Maybe it is my pride, but I convince myself I still don't know this man, whoever he is.

We shake hands and say goodbye.

On the way home, I look at the empty seat next to me. I can't help but feel a sense of loss, and the crushing weight of loneliness. I'm shaken out of my depression by an alert on my phone. I call Barnes Jewish Hospital. My heart sinks even further, and I step on the acceleration pedal.

Within a few miles down the interstate I'm forced to slow down. There is an accident up ahead, further south, and in a few minutes, I find myself stuck in a miles-long traffic jam. Unable to move, I get out my handbag from the back seat hoping there are still some uneaten snacks inside.

A small, leather book falls out. I hadn't journaled in years, but I always kept the little book with me just in case. Instinctively, I untie the leather string and flip to my last entry …

EIGHT
VIVIAN'S CHOICE

Springfield, IL
From Ethan's Journal (five years ago)

July 1st
THIS BOY, THIS BOY will change the world. Like a prophecy, those words echo in my mind. As Vivian and I are faced with the toughest decision of our lives, the words feel more like a promise. There was something special about the child in her nine months-pregnant belly. THIS BOY, this boy will change the world.

The first time she said it, the statue of the Sun Singer was the only other witness, the only other thing with ears to hear. He was like a god to us, that Sun Singer and we were his children. But this boy, this special, unborn boy due to arrive in the world in less than two weeks, this boy, special or not, is now my dilemma, my blessing, and my curse. How can I choose between my wife and my child?

I write this as Vivian sleeps. All was well with the pregnancy, until a few days ago, when it was not. Swollen legs, shortness of breath, fatigue, the symptoms were the same as someone carrying a child. We thought it was normal, didn't think anything was wrong. The doctors said otherwise. They called it peripartum cardiomyopathy, PPCM. I didn't understand much of PPCM, but what I did understand is that

Vivian has a weak heart. She is so calm, so assured, "Trust in God," she says, everything will all work out. I can't be calm. I'm terrified. Fear paralyzes me. What if I must choose?

"This boy," she says as if the answer is obvious. "This boy." The words are like a prayer.

How could this happen? How could God do this to me, to Vivian, to this boy? Get it together, Ethan. Calm down, man. It will all be OK. We have the best doctors. The best medical care. Nothing to do about it now anyway. There is medication, yes, but is it too late? Is there time? All I can do is write, because that's what I do. I write. I write and Vivian prays. She has enough faith for both of us it would seem.

Prayer is hard for me. I do it for her. I pray. I ask. And I ask, and I ask, and I ask. Why? Why? Why!? What do you want? What do you want, God? There is never an answer. To me, prayer is like talking to myself. It doesn't feel like anyone is listening.

Vivian is waking up. Time to go …

July 2nd

At the hospital. Yesterday, after experiencing contractions Vivian went into cardiac arrest at the house. Had to do CPR to get her heart going again. My worst nightmare. Somehow got her into the car and rushed her to the emergency room. Ran every red light, nearly got into a wreck. She must have heard me freaking out in the car. At one point she grabbed my arm and said, "Ask Him, Ethan. Just ask Him."

I knew who she meant. She meant God. Well, trust me darling, I was asking. I was praying like I never prayed before.

Believe it or not, it might have worked too. Vivian was conscious when I pulled up to Memorial. A miracle if you ask me. She is having an emergency C-Section now, but first, the dreaded moment had come. I had to choose. I understood, the doctors had to know just in case. The mother or the baby? It would be fine. They had to ask, right? It was their job. It didn't matter anyway. Vivian came to for just a moment, right before I was going to answer. She looked at me, through the pain she said nothing, and everything. I knew the words. THIS

BOY. THIS BOY, ETHAN. The answer was always there, and I knew it. The decision was already made long ago in the Garden of the Sun Singer. All I can do is wait. All I can do is ask.

July 15th

This boy, this boy is beautiful. His name is Sam. Sam is asleep in my arms. We rock back and forth as I write. Apparently, I can multi-task. Is this what fatherhood is like? Discovering skills you never knew you had?

I can't help but smile as his mouth opens in a yawn. Then tears drop onto the page as I realize he's wanting his mother's milk but will never have it.

Vivian lived long enough to see this boy, long enough to kiss him, to cherish him in the chaos of an operating room.

"This boy," she whispered. And then she died.

Now, this boy will never know her, never see her smile, never feel her presence. This boy will go through life always wondering, "Why?" Why did my life cause my mother's death? This boy will miss what he never knew and yearn for what he never had.

Guilt. I feel guilt. I should feel grateful, but I can't. This boy is here. This beautiful, miraculous boy. But I'm not grateful. I miss Vivian. She's gone. Gone. Gone. Gone. Where is she, now? What is she doing? How can she be dead? She was just here in this bed, in this house. Vivian will always haunt me. Her touch was life. Her voice was meaning.

A life for a life, you say? This boy, this boy can't replace her.

Trust God, she said. Trust HIM, and now she doesn't exist anymore. Well, no more trusting. No more asking. No more praying. I have come to believe we are alone in this world. We make our own way, and no amount of groveling to some distant, invisible Creator will ever change that fact. God is not life. Vivian is life. I could feel her, see her, hear her, smell her. Yes, she is dead. She is not alive, but at least she lived. That's more than God can say.

Tomorrow I will take Sam to our secret place for the first time. It is the place his mother loved more than any other place in the world. It will be my last time there. After July 16th, I will never return to Allerton Park and the Garden of the Sun Singer. It is a place dead to me. The memories there were just an illusion. Without Vivian, the Sun Singer is meaningless. I would tear it down if I could. I hate it. I hate what it means, I hate its memory, I hate what it heard us say, and saw us do. It saw us at our best and at our worst. Left to me, I would melt the Sun Singer, form it into a chain, and drop it to the deepest part of the ocean.

Sam will never know the joy and the pain it caused me. He will never know its memories. His life must be my life now. I must be strong for him. I must be iron-willed. All that is left of Vivian is Sam. His hair is dark like hers, his eyes penetrating and intense, just like hers. I will honor her memory by loving him.

This boy. This boy IS special. There is a knowing in his eyes when he looks at me. I haven't spent a lot of time looking at babies, but this baby can see things. This child will do things the world has never seen before. I will give him a life, a life without a mother, but a life, nonetheless. She will not haunt him; she will make him stronger.

This boy, this boy will live. He will grow. He will become a man and start his own family. Vivian gave him life, so I will give him the strength to live it. I promise you, Vivian. Sam will never want because of me. Our boy will live. Our boy will be happy. Someday, he will bury his father at New Salem, like sons are meant to do. He will not grow weary in doing good. His life will be our life, and he will not fear death. Through struggles and sadness, success and joy, Sam will overcome and live life in the moment. No looking ahead, no looking behind.

And this boy, this boy will bring life to others. I don't know how, and I don't know where or when, but this boy will be a blessing to all mankind. THIS BOY, OUR BOY.

NINE
SERMON ON THE DOZER

Bylas, AZ
September 19th, 2035

DUST SWIRLS AROUND MY feet, whipping up into my eyes, my mouth, and ears, and hair. In this arid desert, the blazing sun is relentless on my head, and there's no shade for miles. Almost two months have passed since I had last seen or heard from Denim Guy. Then, randomly, out of the blue, he asks me to meet him in Arizona at the San Carlos Indian Reservation. I tell him I can be there for a day, but then I have to get back to St. Louis.

We are outside of Bylas, at the site of a huge construction project. Denim Guy is in the seat of a bulldozer moving earth around. He waves to me from the cab with a big smile. The engine shuts off and he hops out.

"One of my favorite things to do," he says, giving me a big hug that nearly lifts me off my feet. He has a yellow neon vest over his denim clothes and a red hard hat.

"What, drive a CAT?" I ask in amusement.

"Operations," he replies. "I have an affinity for projects you know. This is going to be a new health center for the tribe."

Denim Guy points around the site giving me the low-down. The last few months he has visited various reservations, meeting with tribal leaders, helping here and there where he can with First Nations tribes in South Dakota, Oklahoma, Montana, Wyoming, the Northwest, and now here in Arizona.

"I am drawn to these people, Ethan," Denim Guy says of the American Indians, almost in wonder. "A great injustice was done to them, and there have as yet been no reparations to right what was wrong." Another worker arrives and joins us. Denim Guy speaks to him in what I think is fluent Chiricahua ... because, well, because of course. Minutes later the worker returns with a vest and helmet for me to wear.

It was then that a convoy of black SUVs could be seen approaching down US-70, the vehicles shimmering in the sweltering heat.

Denim Guy's demeanor suddenly darkens. "Here come the wolves."

"Wolves? What wolves?"

"Come on," he says with an arm around my shoulder. "Let's get in the CAT before they get here."

There's room enough for me inside the big machine, with a special little seat for a second passenger. Denim Guy starts the engine and begins moving dirt like a pro.

Back at the workers' parking lot, the convoy pulls in. Denim Guy ignores them, but I see five well-dressed white men exit the vehicles, along with a team of videographers and other people. My guess is they are probably personal assistants. Or media producers?

"Who are they?" I ask.

Denim Guy puts the dozer in reverse and looks through the back window. "Wolves," he says dismissively. He looks back at me. "Megachurch pastors who want to know if I am really the Christ."

"Whoever they are, they're walking into the construction site like they own the place."

Over the protest of the site manager—one of the tribal leaders I met when I first arrived—the five men and their entourage march right up to the dozer. Now that they are closer, I do recognize a few of them from TV. Denim Guy shuts off the engine and takes a deep breath. After taking a beat, he opens the door.

"You're back," he says flatly.

"We have questions that need answering," says one of them in a finely-pressed pinstripe suit. "Many of our congregants think you really are Jesus of Nazareth, others aren't sure. There's a lot of concern and confusion. We just want some clarity on a few things. Put to bed the misinformation."

Denim Guy leans out of the cab. "There is no misinformation. I am Jesus of Nazareth. So, what's the problem? What do you want? A miracle? Some kind of sign? Want to see my passport?"

Concerned, the men look at each other. The youngest one has designer shoes, tattoos, and diamond jewelry around his neck and fingers. I can't help but notice he's probably wearing at least fifteen grand in clothes and accessories. He steps forward, briefly stopping to preen for the camera.

"Hi there. My name is Adam. I pastor a church of 40,000 and lead a ministry with a global reach. Some of the most famous, influential people in the world attend my church, and they rely on me to offer them counseling and discernment. To be honest, this is not how the Bible says you would arrive when it describes your Second Coming. We thought you would appear in the air, 'Coming on the clouds with glory,' like it says in Revelation."

"Who says I didn't?" Denim Guy replies. "Maybe you were too busy to notice?"

"Well, excuse me," the young guy says in annoyance. "But the Bible says *every eye* will see him."

"And so, they shall," says Denim Guy. "Even those that pierced me. *When* they see me remains to be seen. How about you? You are seeing me now, yes?"

The young guy laughs nervously. "Well, yes, I suppose." "Scripture is being fulfilled then wouldn't you say?" The men look at each other, uncertain.

"Look," the young man says. "We want to have a conversation with you, get to know you, your theology, and your knowledge of the Bible so that we can confirm you are our Lord and Savior."

"Bullshit," says Denim Guy, and even I am shocked to hear him use such vocabulary. "What you really want is for me to confirm your own theology, and inflate your ego even more, if that is even possible. I will do no such thing."

The five pastors look poleaxed, their jaws on the ground. It didn't look like they were used to being talked down to in such a fashion.

"Well, that proves it then," says another of the five men, a husky fellow in his middle years wearing a leather jacket. "This man is a fake. Another false Christ. Jesus would never use foul language, and he would never scold his servants who have done so much for his kingdom."

"You think you are MY servants building MY kingdom?" Denim Guy gets out of the cab and stands on the tracks of the dozer, towering over the five ministers on the ground. "You prey on the weak to enrich yourselves. Look at you in your fine clothes and jewelry."

"We deserve it!" says leather jacket guy, sweat beading on his forehead. "We have devoted our lives—"

Denim Guy towers over them with a pointed finger, his eyes burning with anger, hurling thunder bolts. "You force your staff and volunteers to sign NDAs. You silence those crying out for justice. You destroy families! Abusers! Thieves! Blind guides, all of you! You intimidate and bully and manipulate people into submission. You lord over them their sins while ignoring your own. You embrace extreme ideologies in my name and profane me." Denim Guy spits in the dirt in disgust.

He turns to the man in the suit. "And you. During the pandemic you kept your church open because of your *'rights'* and allowed the virus to rip through your community, killing hundreds. How is that love? You haven't loved your neighbor, and you haven't given up your *'rights'* for the sake of strangers. Why? Because you wanted fame and prosperity. Because you were afraid you would lose these things if you closed your doors. Shame on you."

He points to the young guy with tattoos. "You twist my words and speak with a forked tongue. You protect your reputation first, and your congregants last. You don't make disciples, you make victims!" He turns to all of them. "Your ministries are an abomination to me. You are a pack of wolves. Go on, then. GO! Publish your books, hold your conferences, rake in your millions. Go! Build your churches. I will go and build mine."

Four of the five men are red-faced with rage at these words. Husky Leather Jacket Dude looks like his eyeballs are about to pop out of his head. A fifth man, short and balding, well, he looks dejected and on the verge of tears.

"It is not I that must prove myself to you," says Denim Guy getting back into the cab. "I AM that I AM. It is you who must prove yourself to me."

"But how?" asks the sullen balding man. He wears a polo shirt and khakis. "Tell me, and I'll do it."

"Don't bother John," says a fourth man in sunglasses and too-tight jeans. "Don't you get it? This isn't Jesus! He's some crazy person, probably possessed by demons. You think the real Jesus would be in the middle of the desert moving dirt around? ON AN INDIAN RESERVATION!? Come on, man. The real Jesus wouldn't be *here*. He'd be at our churches, with us, his people. This guy is a fake."

Denim Guy starts up the dozer and looks directly at the balding fifth man. "You want to know how to prove yourself to me as a true disciple? Here is how: RESIGN from your ministry. Today. This very moment. Become irrelevant and unknown. Serve me quietly, in obscurity, without your lights and cameras and stadiums and adoring followers. Return your excessive wealth to the poor. Then and only then will I know you are a sheep and not a wolf."

The four other men burst into laughter. "Come on, let's get out of here," says Leather Jacket Dude. "What a waste of time." The four stomp off, retreating to the safety of their SUVs as fast as they can without breaking out into a full run.

The guy with no hair looks utterly lost and hopeless. I almost feel sorry for him. He looks at Denim Guy, then back at his four companions, who are joking around as they leave, completely unbothered by what Denim Guy said. Conflicted, Balding Man hesitates, but eventually, he slinks away to join his friends.

Denim Guy slams the door shut. "Like I said ... *wolves*."

"Was that really wise?" I can't help but ask. "Those five men influence a whole lot of people. They are now going to tell the whole world you are a fake."

"Of course, they are," says Denim Guy. "But they were always going to do that. Long ago their hearts hardened against me. It will be very hard for them to enter the kingdom of heaven."

"That's really unfortunate."

"Those five men prey on the weak, and then feast on their souls. They have not in mind the things of God. If someone says 'Look, here is the kingdom' or points to the Bible and says, 'Look, the answer is clear,' when it is not clear, that person is a deceiver. The kingdom cannot be seen in human terms of success. In the wrong hands, right theology can be weaponized to destroy instead of love. My religion is soft and gentle and nurturing and fierce ... like a mother."

"Well," I say, grabbing a handle on the roof of the cabin as I get jostled about, "it sounds nice, better than what I've heard elsewhere. Hey, it's good to see you again."

"Likewise, Ethan," he replies. "How's everything at home?"

"Things are ... hm." I'm not exactly sure how to respond. Denim Guy has never asked me about my personal life before, so I'm a little caught off guard. "Things are rough, to be honest, but let's get back to you. Something you said before got my attention. It was about reparations ..."

"Ah, yes."

"That's kind of a touchy subject here in the States. Some people don't like the idea of bearing the punishment for someone else's sins, or you know, a prior generation's bad conduct and transgressions. But I know you like that kind of thing."

Denim Guy stops the dozer and shuts off the engine. "Bearing the consequences of someone else's sins is the beating heart of Christianity. How do you suppose I ended up on that cross so many years ago?"

"Right. What did you call it before? Solidarity consciousness?"

He leans back in the seat and lets the dozer push dirt up toward the west end of the site. "When we led the Hebrews out of Egypt, we required the current generation of Egyptians to pay reparations for the full 400 years the Hebrews were enslaved. The generation that saw the slaves freed, had to pay for the iniquities of the slaveholders from the past four centuries. In the scriptures there is precedent if someone needs that." He shrugs, folds his arms, and gazes out the window. "To a conservative, this idea will be abominable. So, it seems maybe there is a political implication to your question. Attempts to place me into a political box will never work in the end. The right wing will think I'm a leftist, the leftists will think I am too strict, too old-fashioned. Those in the middle will find me frustrating because I don't stake out a practical middle-ground compromise. Whatever someone thinks I am, I am sure to disappoint them."

"Who decides what is the right amount to pay?" I ask. "In regard to the reparations, that is."

"The solution isn't necessarily practical. It isn't supposed to be. I would ask the ones who have been victimized. Work out a solution. Listen to each other." Denim Guy puts it in reverse and does a three-point turn. "What the white settlers did to the tribes here was a crime against humanity, a crime against God. They murdered and kidnapped and abused their way to the Pacific. Then they gave false witness, broke their treaties, left the First Nations peoples in rags. When the missionaries came and told them about me, they abused them again by forcing the children into boarding schools where the little ones were abused and murdered. Furthermore, they did not allow the tribes to worship me in their own cultural and ceremonial way. The settler missionaries wanted white Christians, not Christians in spirit and truth. So, they tried to make converts to their white culture instead of making my disciples. In many respects the settler missionaries unknowingly shut the door of the Kingdom on my own people, a people for whom I visited, telling them of the whites who would come with a metal cross bearing messages on leaves."

At this point, I need some clarification. "Wait, so you ... *visited* with them? When? How? In what fashion?"

"In visions and dreams. Centuries ago, I appeared to people like Circling Raven and Shining Shirt, and many others whose names are written in the Lamb's Book of Life. I was with them, and I knew them. They were not Christians, but in many ways, they were more Christian than the missionaries. Many First Nations tribespeople worshipped me in spirit and truth. Spiritually, they are well more advanced than the privileged. I have come to free them from the oppression of colonial Christianity.

"Take the African-American community here in the US. If anyone should reject me, it should have been them. For centuries they were enslaved, treated like cattle, worse than livestock, and by people who claimed to follow me, but their power cut through the demonic activity of the white slaveholders and overcame them. They found me. I found them. I was with them always, and they abided in me through it all. I am a God who stands with the oppressed. The oppressor is of the devil, especially when that oppressor oppresses in my name."

"I guess that leads to the ... um." Suddenly I realize that once again I have forgotten to press record on my phone, and once again I find my phone has miraculously already been recording. This is getting ridiculous. Get it together, Ethan.

"The historical question," I continue, trying to get my train of thought. "Was the US founded as a Christian nation?"

"Obviously not," says Denim Guy. "There are no *Christian* nations per se, only nations. And nations do good things, and they do bad things. It is a mistake to idolize nations, even the First Nations people of this land should not be blindly adored. Before the Europeans came, they were not perfect. They were human, and human histories are filled with successes and failures, atrocities and triumphs, good citizens, bad citizens, corrupt officials, and ethical governments. We must honor cultures and societies by affirming their good attributes in the context of their failures and weaknesses."

He finishes building a pad on the site of the new building, or at least that's what I think is going on (I'm not big into construction).

With the dozer parked, we hop out of the cab and make our way to the parking lot.

"Let me ask you something," says Denim Guy as we hand over our PPE to the site supervisor. "If you were me, what would you do?"

"What would I do?" I ask in confusion. "You mean, like right now, or …?"

"If Ethan Tellinger was all-powerful, what would he do in the world today?"

"Oh, um, I don't know …" I think about it for a second. "Probably solve world hunger. Maybe that would be a good start."

Denim Guy rolls up his sleeves. "Shall we, then?" "Wait, what?"

Without warning, he puts his hand on my forehead. The world … *shifts.*

TEN
BREAD OF THE WILDERNESS

September 19th, 2035

STUMBLING BACKWARD, I SHIELD my eyes from the sun and dust. Disoriented, I try to get my bearings. That had to be the strangest sensation I have ever experienced, like the whole world just moved right *through* my body.

"What ... was that?" I say, choking away the dust. "Open your eyes, Ethan," Denim Guy commands.

I do as commanded and can't believe what I'm seeing. The construction site is gone. The dozer is gone. The parking lot, highway 70, the Apache workers, everything and everyone is gone. Only the desert remains, except the desert looks different now. Small bushes dot the sand. The terrain is hilly and rolling.

"Where are we?"

"East Africa," says Denim Guy. "Somalia. Site of the world's greatest famine."

"How ...? No, no, no, no, there's no way, I can't ..." Vertigo sets in.

"Steady yourself, Ethan."

Denim Guy puts an arm around my waste. "Is it really that implausible? After everything you've seen and heard? Space and distance are subject to me. All spaces are the same space. The painter is greater than the paint. Stone is molded by water and air, but where does either come from? What is greater, the chisel, the hammer, or the hands which steady both? This world is but the mold for the new which is coming. Today you will see a glimpse of it."

Instinctively I get out my phone and look for a signal. The global GPS gets a signal. It pins me in Somalia, exactly as Denim Guy said.

"This is, this is crazy," I say in disbelief. A cloud of dust appears on the horizon.

"Look there," says Denim Guy, pointing. "Our ride is approaching."

The *ride* which my companion is referring to is three trucks with machine guns fitted to the back. Stern-faced men in body armor and belts of ammo around their chests occupy the vehicles.

"Militia?"

Denim Guy nods in the affirmative. "The warlord's men. They will take us to the city."

My heart feels like it's about to beat outside of my chest.

"Don't worry, Ethan." Denim Guy pats my shoulder. "Do not fear.

Everything will be A-OK. Trust me, yes?"

Rusted vehicles slide to a halt only feet away from us. Armed men hop out with guns. They are shouting in Arabic. Denim Guy holds up his hands and gets down on his knees. I do the same. Our hands are bound behind our backs, and a black hood is placed over our heads. We are hustled into the back of one of the trucks. I'm terrified and gasping for breath in the stifling hood when the truck suddenly takes off. Is this it? Is this how I die? What will my son do without me? My thoughts spiral into despair. I also feel annoyance, and anger, anger at Denim Guy for putting me in this situation. If he had the power to teleport us here, then getting captured was within his power to prevent. I'm a prisoner on the other side of the world because he wanted me to be.

"Ethan..." I hear a familiar voice say. But the voice isn't heard in my ears. At least I don't think—

"*Ethan, it's me.*"

"*H-hello?*" I respond in my head to the voice. "*Denim Guy? What is this? Telepathy?*"

"*You will not be harmed by these men,*" he says—or … thinks to me … inside my head. "*It's important you trust me. I know you are angry and afraid that I put you in this situation, but this will only last a little while.*"

"*Easy for you to say,*" I respond. "*You have all this power. I'm sure you'll be fine.*"

"*Don't forget, Ethan, I faced death too. I once felt the terror you feel. The anger. The panic. The despair. I experienced it in the Garden of Gethsemane, just before they came to take me away to the Sanhedrin, and then to Pilate, and eventually, to the cross. You are not alone, just as I was not alone in the Garden.*"

The idea of Almighty God being terrified seemed ludicrous to me. How would that even be possible? Even so, what was the point of all this? Denim Guy isn't like me. He doesn't know. He doesn't know that it isn't MY death that scares me. But the death of my son? My only child—

"*This boy,*" Denim Guy whispers inside my brain.

"I have to go home!" I scream through my hood. I am overcome with fear. "Please! My son needs me!"

One of the guards shouts at me. Something hits me in the head. Warm blood trickles through my hair. Dizzy, I fall over. My sense of awareness fades, and then … nothing.

Light. Blinding light. My eyes squint, trying to adjust out of the darkness. I realize we're not in the truck anymore but outside a decrepit, mixed-use building. I'm on the ground and Denim Guy is knelt beside me.

He helps me to my feet. "The worst is over, Ethan." "Where are we?"

"Mogadishu." Denim Guy dusts off my clothes. "We are going to see the warlord now."

"How long have you known my son is terminally ill?"

"I have always known, Ethan Tellinger." He slips my phone into my pocket.

Of course. I open my mouth to respond, but the point of a gun is shoved into my lower back, and we are escorted by the guards into the building. There is trash and old furniture scattered around haphazardly. We go up a flight of crumbling stairs that creak and bow as we ascend. Directed through a set of double doors and into a large conference room, I see a bald man with a crown and sunglasses smoking a cigar on what looks to be an elevated makeshift throne. Scantily clothed, depressed-looking women sit at his feet.

The guns in our backs push us toward the throne and the warlord sitting on it. He blows a smoke ring and lets out a booming laugh.

"Forever Man!" The warlord gloats. "The most WANTED man, in the world. I knew God would reward me today. And he gave me an American too. Blessings everywhere, yes?"

I look to Denim Guy, but he says nothing. He just stands there, staring at the warlord, calm and expressionless.

"Are you happy to see me Forever Man?" asks the warlord. He yanks one of the women onto his lap. "What do you think of my kingdom?"

Denim Guy steps forward. "The time for glorying in yourself has come to an end, Farouk."

The warlord laughs again. "Take them to the prison cells," he says to the guards. The armed men snap into action. They move forward to take us, but suddenly, without warning, they drop their weapons and fall to the ground, completely unconscious.

"What is this?" snaps the warlord Farouk. "Get up you fools! Take them away!"

The guards lie still.

"They are sleeping only," says Denim Guy. "The best sleep they have ever had. In fact, all your soldiers and lieutenants are sleeping, all 15,000 men and boys who fight for you have been rendered helpless. You are the king of nothing now, Farouk."

Farouk pulls out a radio and calls for backup in Arabic. "Aziz? Aziz! Mohammed?" No one responds. The warlord chuckles. "Well, aren't you full of surprises Mr. Forever Man?"

Denim Guy looks to the women around the throne. "You are free to go. Nothing will happen to you," he says to them. The women look at each other, uncertain. Realizing their newfound freedom, they bolt out of the room.

"Hey!" Farouk screams in rage at the women. "Come back here!" He turns to Denim Guy. "Those belonged to me. Who do you think you are?"

"The King of Kings," Denim Guy responds quietly. He walks up to the dais and calmly removes Farouk's crown. He tosses it to the ground. "You a have woman held in captivity here. Her name is Phoebe. I want to see her."

Farouk laughs nervously. "The whore? Ah, is that what this is about? You wanted some alone time with a woman? Well, why didn't you say so my friend? Are you sure you want Phoebe, though? My men have already been through her, why not someone more fresh?"

The former warlord is lifted out of his throne in thin air like a ragdoll. "OK, OK! Put me down. I'll take you to her."

Denim Guy pulls out a note from his pocket. "Call this number, Ethan. Tell the republic forces and UN peacekeepers that they can now enter the city. The drones and satellites will give them confirmation."

I call the number. It takes a moment for the other side of the line to find an English speaker, but eventually, it gets sorted.

Farouk leads us out of the throne room and down to the basement, from which comes the most hideous smell I have ever encountered. I can't help but cover my nose as we pass sleeping guards, and through a hallway of locked cells. Denim Guy opens each locked cell, nearly ripping the hinges off the doors. Shocked and emaciated prisoners flee. At the end of the corridor, we come to the last cell. I cannot even describe in words the odor and appearance of the cells.

"Here is the woman," Farouk mutters. "Phoebe." He unlocks the door. A naked woman is on the floor of the cell. She is curled in a fetal position.

Tears stream down Denim Guy's face as he begins to unbutton his shirt. He takes it off and drapes the shirt over the naked woman.

"Come here, Farouk." Denim Guy motions for him to enter. "You will now face justice for your crimes."

Gently, Denim Guy picks up Phoebe and carries her out of the cell. With his foot, he slams the door shut with Farouk locked inside.

"Forever Man!" Farouk shouts, banging on the door. "You cannot leave me here! What about forgiveness? What about your mercy? Let's make a deal, you and me! Let's reason together!"

The sound of his protests and belly-aching fades away as we leave the jail; without a doubt, the worst place I have ever been. A shirtless Denim Guy cradles Phoebe in his arms and delivers her from this nightmare. Outside, we commandeer one of the militia vehicles. I get in the driver's seat, and see my personal things are there waiting for me. Denim Guy gets in the truck bed, still holding Phoebe. I start the engine. In the rear-view mirror, I see a dazed Phoebe transfixed on the man holding her in his arms, her matted brown hair blowing in the wind around his calm, stern face.

I start the engine. Not sure where to go, I pick the widest street and head west, into the setting sun. Armored personnel carriers pass us as we leave Mogadishu, the soldiers inside confused by the sleeping militia on the streets and the sudden change of events.

Miles outside the city, we pull into a United Nations Reception Camp. Emergency Services take Phoebe into their care. She is dehydrated and malnourished, suffering from a concussion and a few broken ribs. Several hours later we are allowed to visit her in a tent. She is hooked up to an IV and currently asleep. Denim Guy recovers his shirt and puts it on.

"What will happen to her?" I ask, curious to know this woman's fate. She was, in fact, not a prostitute, but a nun, one of the Missionaries of Charity, here working as a nurse. "Does she become some great leader in the future?"

"That is your Western way of thinking coming through," Denim Guy says, buttoning his shirt, barely hiding his contempt.

"Meaning …?"

"The idea that horrible things only happen for some greater

purpose. Sometimes there is just suffering with no greater purpose other than to bear it and keep on living. What do you want me to say? That Phoebe will become a great spiritual icon? A world-famous award-winning symbol of peace to the nations? That many will follow me through her testimony and teaching because of what she suffered here? Her future is not yet determined. Her trauma will remain, but I will sustain her. A quiet life is a great life, Ethan. I dwell in the obscure, simple rhythms, and duties of life: unwashed dishes, dirty laundry, loud children running around the house."

I rub my temples. "OK look, that's all great to hear, but I really do need to get home."

"Yes, back to your son." Denim Guy tucks in his shirt and studies my face. "How long has he been ill?"

"I suppose you already know. So why ask?"

"I want to hear it from you," Denim Guy answers.

Whatever. "Several years ago, I realized something wasn't right. He was pale, no energy, no appetite. They did lots of tests. Eventually, Sam was diagnosed with a rare and incurable blood disorder. I should say, it's incurable for now. There are always new treatments to explore."

"Which led you to me," says Denim Guy. A breeze ripples the tent fabric and Phoebe stirs. "I'm very sorry Ethan. Why don't you—"

"It doesn't matter. You've done all these great things, but it still doesn't prove you are who you say you are."

"True," says Denim Guy. "Nevertheless, you cannot deny the miracles you've seen. So why don't you ask me?"

Again, with this. Over and over. I give up. "All right, fine. Can you heal my son? WOULD you heal my son?"

"No."

That word, spoken without hesitation, hits me in the chest. I can't help but laugh. "Right, of course. Why? Why did you want me to ask then? I believe you can do it. So do it!"

"Ethan …"

He reaches for my shoulder but I back away. "What kind of a God wouldn't heal a sick child? You're just a cruel son of a bitch. Stringing me along, getting my hopes up. Then Boom! Rejection. Well, fuck you. Suffering isn't a divine privilege you prick. Suffering sucks. It's terrible. That's what I know." The more I think about it, the more it makes me angry. I start pacing around the tent.

"Ethan—"

"I get it. You don't owe me anything. You're not a genie. I don't have three wishes to be granted. But come on, my only boy … my child, he doesn't deserve this … I can't bury my son."

"Ethan, ask me again."

I wipe the tears from my cheeks. "What? Why would I do that? You just said you wouldn't do it. Oh, wait. You want me to beg? You want me to NEED you, is that it? Well, what's that going to do? Either heal my son, or don't."

Visibly disappointed, Denim Guy lowers his head. "I have compassion for you Ethan. I will sustain you and your son. I know you cannot understand my ways, not yet. A day is coming when you will. For now, know this." He takes my face into his hands. "I will never give up asking you to ask me."

"This is so stupid," I comment. And it is. Spiritual hokey pokey was idiotic.

"You HAVE spoken truly," he continues. "Suffering sucks, as you say. I feel you. Your pain is my pain. All over the world, children are dying. My children, the owners of my Kingdom, my precious ones. These same children, they die of disease and hunger and neglect and violence. The world despises them, but you must become like them. I do not care, Ethan, about people becoming very great, or very wise, or very spiritual, or prosperous and happy. I want everything on a small scale. Become a good little child, and you will abide in me. You will inherit a share of what is coming."

"Which is …?"

He lets go of my face. "I told you before, I have come to create a new world. Things are about to change. There is to be an Awakening, a holy fire, spreading across the world. All that is needed is a spark to light the flame, a piece of bread cast upon the waters."

More riddles. "Sure, great. What kind of Awakening are you talking about here?"

Denim Guy sits next to Phoebe and holds her hand. "As it is written: *'You who dwell in the dust, awake and sing for joy.'*"

The tent flap opens. It's our old acquaintance from the UN, silver-haired Ibrahim. He embraces Denim Guy and shakes my hand.

"Did you hear?" Ibrahim asks in excitement. "We have re-taken the city. The militia has been induced into some kind of coma, a deep sleep. They are being rounded up as I speak. And Farouk! Farouk was found locked in his own jail."

"That is great to hear," Denim Guy replies. "Right, Ethan?"

"But what about you?" Ibrahim asks. "I saw you on TV with the Pope. How on earth did you end up here?"

Neither I nor Denim Guy say anything.

"Well, never mind," Ibrahim says, sensing the subject is off-limits. "There is still much more work to do here. I better get going."

"Right, the famine." Denim Guy stands up. "Shall we get to it then?"

I look at Ibrahim. Ibrahim looks at me. Denim Guy leaves the tent, and we follow. Outside, the camp is buzzing with activity. Emergency relief workers are moving about, helping refugees. The UN base is really the entrance to a greater refugee camp, a collection point for people fleeing Ethiopia, Djibouti, Sudan. Denim Guy walks into the refugee camp. Hundreds of white tents stretch into the distance. Countless scores of East Africans see Denim Guy and immediately flock to him. The adults mill around unsure and curious, but the children are fearless. Starving, half-naked boys and girls run up to Denim Guy smiling and laughing. All of them are reaching out to touch him.

"Hallelujah! Hallelujah Forever Man!" they cry, and before too long the adults follow the lead of the children. Some gather around in celebration and praise; most simply fall face down where they stand as Denim Guy passes. What a scene. I have never witnessed anything like this before.

And it doesn't stop as we move through the camp. Word spreads.

Other refugees come to see The Forever Man, and not just see him, they come to *worship* him. Among the shouts of praise and worship and reaching hands, Denim Guy stops and tilts his head toward the cloudless sky. His eyes are closed, and a serene expression is on his brown face.

White specks of dust begin to fall all around us. I hold out my hand. Snow? The pale flakes aren't cold. I look up at the sky. The floating white objects become larger and heavier. Soon there is a snowfall happening all over the camp, except the snow isn't snow. The refugees gasp in awe. I get out my phone and record a video.

"Manna," Ibrahim says, inspecting a piece of the white stuff in his hand. He pops it into his mouth. "Manna from heaven." He gives me a piece and I eat it.

"It's good," I say. "Sweet, and filling. Is this … is this really happening?"

I suddenly realize how quiet things have become in the camp. I look around at the people. The refugees aren't cheering anymore because they're eating! The white bread falls even heavier, inches of it covering the ground, the tents, the people. The whole camp, moments before in a desolate wasteland, now looks like it belongs on a postcard, a veritable winter wonderland. Even the temperature of the air has cooled. The white stuff is in our hair and on our clothes. Children begin to do snow angels on the ground. They form balls of the manna and laugh as they have a manna-ball fight.

Denim Guy calmly walks over to us.

"You're doing this?" I ask him, already knowing the answer.

"I am the bread of life." Denim Guy takes a piece of manna and eats it. "The Good Shepherd. I will feed my sheep." He looks up overhead. Flocks of birds fly over us. They descend on the camp.

"Look!" says Ibrahim. "Quail! It is the Book of Exodus all over again."

Water spurts up from the ground in a geyser. People fetch pans and buckets to fill.

"From now on," says Denim Guy. "Wherever there is hunger and thirst, manna will fall and water will emerge afresh every day." The water will flow to the sea and back again. The quail will come too. Orchards will grow. This will happen wherever there is need, wherever there is famine. No one will be hungry. No one will be thirsty."

"This is ... This—" I try to form words, but none come to mind. I really don't know what to say. I feel a sense of wonder, but also resentment. A person who could do this could easily heal a dying child. Denim Guy healed that Palestinian boy, but he wouldn't heal Sam.

Denim Guy looks at me and smiles. "THIS is a new world," he says. There is still tension between us, but for now, we watch the people eat and celebrate. The children play in the manna and water. They are delighted when Denim Guy joins in the fun. He scoops them up in his arms and tosses them up in the air. He runs around us laughing as the children throw balls of manna at his back. For the first time in their lives, they are full and content. Whatever future Denim Guy had planned for the world ... it belonged to them first.

ELEVEN
MOVER OF MOUNTAINS

Kyiv, Ukraine December 1st, 2035

TWO MONTHS LATER, THE world has transformed ... is still *being* transformed to put it more accurately. Denim Guy has now rearranged the global order. He is the most famous person on earth. With the blessing of the Pope and other faith traditions, his followers now number in the billions. Poverty has nearly been eradicated. The spread of disease has nearly disappeared. There is abundance everywhere in the world. Things are going well for him, and me too. Sam has responded well to a new treatment. His strength has returned, and he is in good spirits. Despite all the good news, conflict remains, which leads us to now. For the third time in thirteen years, Russia is threatening to invade Ukraine. Everyday more troops and tanks and supply vehicles arrive across the border. It is an invasion force 500,000 strong. An army designed for one thing. Annihilation.

For a few days I have agreed to join Denim Guy on this mission to Ukraine. Snow-dusted pine trees pass by as we look out the window of our train heading east to Kyiv. My companion, still dressed in his original blue shirt and jeans from the refugee camp, sits opposite me in the train car. Freezing, I am bundled up in a coat and earmuffs, but Denim Guy seems unbothered by the chill. A select entourage of nuns and other women follow him wherever he goes now. The ladies, called the Sisters of Christ, fill the rest of the carriage and chat amongst themselves.

"Do not be fooled, Ethan." Denim Guy studies me as I get out my phone.

"Fooled?"

"Remember," he continues. "The gate is small. It is true what they say. Billions now claim to follow me, but my actual followers are few."

"Please don't do the mind-reading thing. It creeps me out." Using my teeth, I pull off one of my gloves and check my email. There's an alert from the AP that Russia is threatening a tactical nuke strike on eastern Ukraine.

"What is it?" Denim Guy asks. From a duffel bag he pulls out what looks to be the beginnings of a dark blue blanket. He also gets out a crochet hook, pin, scissors, a ball of yarn, and then begins knitting.

"Russia," I respond. "They're threatening to nuke Ukraine." "Those billions," Denim Guy says, I guess going back to his train of thought as if I hadn't just delivered very concerning geopolitical news. He hooks a strand of yarn around the crochet hook. "They follow me because of the miracles, not because I am who I say I am. Others know who I am, and they hate me because of it."

"If they are following you then what difference does it make?" I delete a few spam emails.

"The heart makes all the difference." Denim Guy stretches his back. "These women here, I have done nothing for them, but they would follow me to the ends of the earth. Some do follow me through the miracles, their eyes see, but most people don't care who I am, they only care about what I can do for them."

I decide to leave the last remark alone, and not respond.

"The mark of the righteous," he continues, "is not prosperity, but rather, affliction. The way up is down. All who follow me will face struggles. Just as the Israelites had to descend below the sea to be delivered, so also Peter had to descend below the sea, so I could lift him up again. The downtrodden, the despised, those are my people. The world hates them, wants to use them, always has it been this way. The Romans, they would kidnap people with physical deformities and sell them to the rich, who would then keep them as pets. They would do their buying and selling at places called *monster* markets. Especially popular were hunchbacks, who were thought to bring a household good luck."

"Wow, that's uh ... dystopian, and cruel."

Denim Guy leans forward, his face simultaneously serious and compassionate. "Ethan, I want to adopt all the monsters at the monster market. They will not be my pets; they will be my family. They will inherit what is mine. Their beliefs will flow from their actions in following me. No one will call them hypocrites because their orthopraxy will precede their orthodoxy. In so doing they abide in me and I in them."

The train conductor comes over the intercom to announce we are entering the outskirts of Kyiv.

"But they must bear fruit," he continues. "Without fruit there is no salvation. Many believe once they are saved, they are always saved. But they forget John 15:2: *My Father will cut off every branch IN me that bears no fruit.* In the West, my father has been cutting off many branches. If a person is in me, a regenerated follower, it might not occur to them that my father would be the one to cut them off, but he does. If there is no love, joy, peace, patience, gentleness, kindness, generosity, faithfulness, or self-control, then there is no need for them to be considered my follower. Their connection to me will be cut off."

My phone clicks off and I rub my eyes. "I can see this is all very important to you."

He gives me an eyebrow lift. "Indeed. I also don't want you to be misled by the effect I am having in the world, or by what is next to come. I am a soft and quiet man at heart. I do not gravitate toward machismo or displays of dominance. Patriarchy was part of the curse after Adam fell, it is the old passing away before the new. You have seen me do great wonders, but to live quietly, to nurture and love, these are greater wonders."

The train comes to a stop. "All finished," says Denim Guy holding up the blanket. "What do you think?"

"Very nice."

We disembark, along with the Sisters of Christ. A bus is waiting for us at the station. It's our transportation to the undisclosed location where Denim Guy will meet with the President of Ukraine, and the other Balkan leaders. We are seated on the bus, ready to go, except Denim Guy. He is outside chatting up the bus driver while a media gaggle takes pictures. I look at my watch. We're going to be late. I knock on the window. Denim Guy looks up at me and I tap my wrist. He nods and waves me off. There was no use trying to push him. The Forever Man moved on his own time. The bus driver gives Denim Guy a hug.

By the time he finally gets in the bus, it's only five minutes before our meeting. We rumble down the street, and through the center of Kyiv. The Sisters are dropped off at a hotel. We continue to the undisclosed location. Near an underpass, Denim Guy calls for the bus driver to stop.

I rub my temples in frustration. "You know, we're already late." Denim Guy grabs his new blanket. "This will just take a moment." My eyes roll back into my head. "Sure, take all the time you need."

He hops out of the bus and walks up to the underpass. Climbing to the crevasse where the bridge joined the concrete below, I see Denim Guy wrap the blanket around a homeless person and point to some place off in the distance. There's some kind of conversation going. The homeless person, an old man with a messy shock of white hair, sits up and rubs his eyes. After about fifteen minutes Denim Guy is back on the bus.

"What was that all about?" I ask, expecting some kind of legitimate, earth-shattering explanation that necessitated us holding up anxious world leaders whose countries were about to be invaded any minute.

"He was cold," Denim Guy replies.

"That's it?" Flabbergasted, I decide to the drop the subject. We ride along in silence. When we arrive at the undisclosed location it is an hour past the meeting time. Inside a concrete building we take an elevator down several floors below the surface.

The President of Ukraine is there to greet us, along with the Presidents of Lithuania, Belarus, Estonia, Latvia, and Finland.

"Welcome, Forever Man," says the Ukrainian President. "It is so good to see you."

The four men and three women go into a conference room where intense discussions are taking place. I wait outside with other staff and media and pass the time by scrolling through my phone. About thirty minutes in, Denim Guy pops his head out of the conference room and motions for me to come inside.

Maps cover a large table where the leaders are gathered. They speak in hushed tones and look at me side-eyed with suspicion. The Russians had been posing their spies as journalists, so I do not find this surprising.

Based on the look of their faces, the situation was dire. As I sit down at the table, the maps are quickly rolled up so I can't see their contents. "Once again the Russian Bear is causing trouble," says Denim Guy with a commanding tone. He knows how to control a room when he wants to. "But I am creating a new world, a world without war."

"We have to defeat the Russians first," says the leader of Finland. "Only through victory can there be peace." The woman sits back in her chair with a furrowed brow of determination.

"They intend to invade all of us," says a stocky man in a gray jacket. "And it will be different this time. The Russians learned from 2022. They are smarter, and they have reinforcements from China, and Saudi. Their force is now staged all the way up the Balkans, to the border of Finland. If they attack, it will be World War III."

"They won't attack," says Denim Guy. "This is not the Last Battle. Not yet. Have the towns along the border been evacuated?"

The leaders confirm all border towns with Russia are vacant. The President of Ukraine points on the map which he has unfolded, seemingly forgetting that I am here. Maybe because The Forever Man has vouched for me then it is OK? "Civilians have been moved back to here. Our forces have positions here, here, and here, all along the border. Do you think they should move?"

Denim Guy shakes his head. "That will not be necessary. I will move them with the land, along with everything else."

The leaders look at each other in confusion.

"My English is not the best," says the Finnish woman. "Did you say …"

"I will also adjust the GPS systems for private and commercial flights to land safely," Denim Guy muses to himself, his head cocked to the side. "The pipelines and energy grids have already been disconnected, so there is no need to worry about those. Everything will move as one."

"GPS systems?" asks the President of Ukraine. "Pipelines?"

"Yes, and yes, you heard me correctly, Jaana." Denim Guy takes a seat and relaxes. "Not a single shot will be fired. I will make a wall for you, a buffer, to keep that troublesome Bear away."

"But *how* will you do this?" asks the Estonian president, a woman in her fifties with long blonde hair. Her face is a picture of skepticism as it looks to The Forever Man for an answer.

Denim Guy points to a place on one of the maps. "Take me here, Mount Uzdyhalnytsya, the place where lovers make their oaths, and I will show you."

Uncertainty, and maybe exasperation, covers the faces of the leaders. They seem disappointed by the great Forever Man. Nevertheless, transportation is arranged, and the site is prepared for a visit of the six leaders and Denim Guy. Hours later we are ascending Mount Uzdyhalnytsya in central Kyiv, along with a few local media, government aids, advisors, security guards, and the Sisters of Christ. At or near the top Denim Guy looks out over the city to the east. After a moment, he closes his eyes and holds out his hand palm upward.

I notice the leaves falling first. Then it feels like I'm losing balance. Suddenly, the earth begins to shake. First it was a slight tremor, but the more Denim Guy's hand lifted higher, the more the shaking increased. Pandemonium breaks out on the Mount, security hunkers down with the leaders, covering them from any falling branches, though none fall. A few Sisters scream in fear, but for the most part they stand steady.

Denim Guy's hand lifts higher. Under our feet the ground lets out a hollow moan so loud we cover our ears. It's as if the very earth itself is crying out in pain.

"Make it stop!" I yell at Denim Guy, but to no avail. Not even I can hear my own voice in the tumult of the earthquake. The moaning and rumbling intensify and reach a high-pitched crescendo. Denim Guy's hand is now lifted directly above his head.

I crawl over to where he is standing. Grabbing onto his legs, I hold on for dear life. This close to him, I feel the power emanating out of his body. It is both terrifying and soothing at the same time. Feeling steadier this close to Denim Guy, I stand up, my arms clutched around his waist like I'm riding behind him on a motorcycle.

And then. Silence. The shaking stops, just as suddenly as it started.

Miraculously, the landscape doesn't appear all that different.

Denim Guy pats my arm, looking at me over his shoulder with a grin. "You OK there, Ethan?"

"Wha ... what—"

Cell phones start ringing all over the Mount. Bewildered aids and security guards look at their devices in astonishment. Calls start to pour in. The world leaders speak on their satellite phones, their voices hushed with wonder and fear. Some of them are shouting, but it's not in English so I don't know what's going on.

The president of Ukraine runs over. "Mountains," he says, completely stunned. "There are mountains all along our eastern border. The Generals, they claim they just ... appeared out of the ground. Forever Man, what did you—"

Denim Guy walks past the president, and over to the Sisters, leaving me standing alone with the president of Ukraine. We look at each other, our mouths hanging open.

The Finnish president comes over to us. "A mountain range has appeared on our eastern border. Just ... *appeared* ... out of the earth. All the towns and villages have been pushed to the side. There are no reports of injuries." She covers her mouth and looks at her phone in disbelief.

Reports continue to pour in. It was the same with Latvia and Estonia and Belarus. A new mountain range has just risen out of the earth in minutes, and it was not just any mountain range. These mountains were 9,000 meters high, higher than the Himalayas, they stretched from the Kerch Strait and the northwestern tip of the Caucasus Mountains, all the way to the Norway/Russian border in the Arctic Circle. Over 2,500 miles of impassable mountains that are 150 miles wide.

"Not a single building has been damaged," Denim Guy says to the leaders. "Not one person has been injured or killed. Everyone and everything have moved with the land. We are now roughly 75 miles west of where we were a few minutes ago. On the other side, Asia is now about 75 miles east of where they were. Their missiles will now be easy to shoot down. I have raised these mountains to push the continents apart so that they will protect you. From now on, you will be separated from your abuser."

Denim Guy walks over to me, his gaze intent and compassionate. "As it is written: *They shall beat their swords into plowshares, and their spears into pruninghooks: nation shall not lift up sword against nation, neither shall they learn war anymore.*"

TWELVE
DREAMWALKER

January 15th, 2036

SUNLIGHT WARMS MY FACE. A faint breeze ruffles my hair. I lay on my back in tall grass. With my finger, I trace the outline of puffy white clouds floating above me. If I didn't know any better, I would think this might be heaven. But where is Sam? There's no heaven without my Sam. The sound of children playing is heard some distance away. No, not children, a child. I sit up and see Sam running through the grass. Denim Guy is there with him. They're flying a kite. I feel a knot in my chest and realize this isn't real. I'm asleep in my bed in St. Louis, and this is a dream.

Oh well, might as well enjoy it while it lasts. I watch Sam run and play. What I wouldn't give for this to be a reality, but no, Sam is back in his bed where he spends most of his time because he is too weak to play, too weak to run, too weak to be a kid.

I lay back down in the grass. Hard to say how much time passes in a dream. I go back to the clouds for a while. A shadow hovers over me. I feel it more than I see it in this fuzzy, shifting place of dreamland. Shielding my eyes, I see the blurry visage of Denim Guy standing over me. "Fancy meeting you here," he says.

"Not now," I grumble. "Bother me in the waking world if you

could, please. Just let me dream." I shoo him away with my hand. He sits down next to me in response.

"We're both dreaming," says Denim Guy.

I prop myself up with an elbow. "Wait, you are actually ... *here*, in my dreams?"

"Yes," he replies. "So is Sam. We are all sharing the same dream."

"That is so ... weird." I wave to Sam. He waves back. "So, um, where are you in the waking world?" I ask.

"China. I thought I would pop in and say hello."

"Oh, right. Well ... hello. My dreams aren't usually like this. Usually, I'm fighting something, or someone is chasing me, and I can't get away. Very cliché."

"Dreams are healthy." Denim Guy crosses his legs. "Good dreams, bad dreams, weird dreams, the dreamworld grounds the mind."

"If you say so. How are you doing in China, Dream Denim Guy?"

"Lately, I have been sad. Sometimes I cry a lot. Being all-knowing and all-powerful can do that to you."

It seemed an odd notion to me. "God can be ... sad?"

"God is a Man of Sorrows, Ethan Tellinger." Denim Guy tilts his head as if recalling a memory. "But there is a joy in the midst of sorrow, a joy you can't find anywhere else. Psalm 84: *Blessed are those whose strength is in you, whose hearts are set on pilgrimage. As they pass through the Valley of Weeping, they make it a place of springs.*"

"Believe me, I know all about the Valley of Weeping."

"Yes, the Valley is a valley. You know, it's OK to not feel well. It's OK to be tired. Sometimes, spiritual answers, though they may be true, can be oppressive. Often, I am hesitant to speak. I am listening to the heart. People are complex. They can be hurt while healing, broken while being made whole, alive, yet dying, righteous and still sinning, at war, yet always at peace, hungry, but filled, burdened, and relieved, ransomed, yet taken captive, carriers of death and carriers of life. So, I say, come to me all you who are weary and burdened. I will give you rest. My yoke is easy and my burden light."

"That's a bit contradictory if you ask me." I glance at him out of the corner of my eye. "Which I know you are not, asking, that is."

"The yoke and burden are mandatory. If you are not yoked, and you are not burdened, well, then you are not following me. My hope is that people are burdened with my burdens. Yoked with my yoke. These are peace and comfort."

"Self-confident people have peace, in my experience."

"And what is so attractive about a self-confident person?" Denim Guy responds. "It isn't their confidence. It's their peace, even if it's a false peace. Peace is attractive. My yoke and my burden are light, but it isn't light for you. It's light for me, and if I am *in* you, then my yoke and my burden will be light *for* you. My people can take up my burdens because they are my body, and individually they are members of it. So, only as a member of my body is my yoke and burden light, peaceful you might say."

"Hm, OK."

"I find it amusing," Denim Guy smiles to himself. "Many Christians mistakenly think the Law was burdensome to the Jews. But it wasn't! I even said it wasn't in Leviticus. Ah, if only people would read the book. The rules and the regulations were not burdensome. People could keep them. The Jews did keep them. The Law only became burdensome when I came along, fulfilled the Law, and said that obeying the rules was no longer good enough. Not murdering someone is not good enough anymore. From now on, even *thinking* about committing murder is to be a murderer. A flash of anger at your neighbor can be murder. To fantasize about adultery is to be an adulterer. Now, if you even imagine sin, you have committed sin."

"Yeah, I would say that's burdensome. No way anyone can live up to that."

"And yet my burden is light, because in me, anyone can do this, but apart from me, they can do nothing."

"Seems like you really glorify weakness, or weak people. But as you are probably aware, Western society glorifies healthy people."

"The body is meant for the Lord, and the Lord for the body," Denim Guy says, sounding like he is quoting someone again.

"What kind of body do I seek? Come to me, all you who are weary and burdened. Notice what I did not say. I did not say come to me all you who have a BMI under 30. I did not say, come to me all you who have it all together, who are mentally fit and gifted and cancer-free. No, I seek tired bodies, worn out souls, anxious minds, depressed hearts. My church is a church of weak people because it is only weak people who can carry my yoke and my burden. The strong won't carry it. Why? If it's too light, not worth their time. If it's too heavy, then still they will believe it won't benefit them correctly. The healthy find it too easy or too hard. You ever see big bodybuilders lifting the small five-pound weights? For the powerful, if something is light, then they think it is simple and not worth much."

"You've lost me."

"In other words, it is only the weary and the weak who can appreciate light burdens and easy yokes. So, I say, come to me all you who are weak. I want YOU. I want your frail body and distraught mind. I value them. They are fitting for the Lord. They are appropriate for what I have to offer. And if the weak come to me, I do not necessarily make them strong. That's an oversimplification. More specifically, I say I will make them a part of myself, which is by nature strong. I want to carry my burden through *you*. With my yoke and my burden, there is no pressure to succeed or be some great history maker. My yoke is a yoke of small things. It is a *cup of water* yoke."

A question comes to mind. "What even is a yoke? Such a weird word. Yoke. Yyyyoke."

"In the Bible, a yoke was an emblem of suffering and affliction and punishment. Imagine then how startling it was for the people who were weary that *another* yoke could give them rest!"

"You and your riddles."

"And my burden? My burden is the obligation to love one another. No longer do you need to compete and compare. No longer do you need to live up to a cultural standard of beauty and success. Those things are not your burden anymore. In me, your burden is to love, because I first loved you. The old debts are gone. I give a new debt:

love one another. This debt is not bondage. It is freedom. There is freedom in debt. Follow me, and you incur more debt, not less."

"Freedom *in* debt?" Sounds bizarre to me. "We are all trying to get out of debt, not in debt."

"Which is why you have to count the cost of following me."

It is starting to sink in now. Whoever or whatever Denim Guy was, the costs of even being associated with him are becoming more apparent. The requirements are all so counter-intuitive.

Speaking of which. "I think part of the problem with your message, especially nowadays, is that social media doesn't engender the kind of qualities in people that you are seeking. People don't want to be weak online, or anywhere else. They want to argue and be contrarian. They want their opinions confirmed. They want to dominate. It makes them feel powerful, which is what people really like. Power. Social media was designed to bring out in people the opposite of what you want or value."

"Social media brings out in people what is already there," Denim Guy replies. "You just aren't used to seeing it, but I've seen it since the Garden of Eden and the Tower of Babel. Realize, it's not like if social media did not exist, then people wouldn't have hate in their heart. People have hate in their heart, so social media exists as it is today, *mostly* a hate-filled place. It can also be a place of love and friendship and polite debate. But keyboards and pens have killed more people than swords and bombs. All the great atrocities of the world are first reduced into writing before they are ever reduced to action. Invasions, genocides, wars, the Holocaust, racism, systematic injustice, oppression, in almost all cases, these begin with a stroke of a pen or tap of a keyboard."

"Fair enough," I say. Sam runs over to me and falls into my lap. "Sam, do you know who this is sitting next to me?"

"It's Jesus," Sam says, matter-of-fact. "He always visits me here. Sometimes we play baseball with the angels. I hit a home run last time! We'll fly a kite like today or go fishing. If we have enough players, we'll play football. You were there too, Dad, but I know you don't always remember your dreams like I do."

"Is that so?" I look to Denim Guy.

He ruffles Sam's hair. "We make a pretty good team, yeah?"

Now I know this really is just a dream. Sam playing ball with Jesus and angels? Huh. Too good to be true. I come back down to earth. My brain is trying to process everything that has happened these last six months. This wasn't just a dream; it was a fantasy. It could never be real. Reality was stress and confusion and more stress.

I catch Denim Guy staring at me. "One thing before you wake up …"

My surroundings start to get hazy and muddled like they do in dreams right before they end.

"What is it?" I ask.

"Ask me," says Denim Guy. "Don't give up. Ask me, and ask me, and ask me again."

I blink my eyes awake in my bedroom. It's a little after 3 am. I check on Sam in his room. He's asleep. The homecare life alert machine beeps as it monitors his oxygen and heart rate. Just as I close the door, I notice a small smile at the corner of his mouth.

I pause at the door and wonder. "Could it be?" I ask myself. "No, no, just a dream, Ethan. Get it together."

THIRTEEN
THE STORY OF MOXIE, LISA, AND PAUL

Los Angeles, CA March 3rd, 2036

IT'S MIDNIGHT. I'M TIRED, hungry, and irritated. My bedtime at the latest is usually around 9:30 pm, at least when I'm home. Weeks after Ukraine, I get a message from Denim Guy. He says to meet him here, at the Neverland Nightclub, one of the most exclusive, swanky clubs in Los Angeles. We're here to meet someone, although he doesn't say who. Whatever can be said of Denim Guy, God or no God, he never ceases to surprise.

Neverland is in West Hollywood, in a sprawling renovated commercial building. I've been standing in line to get in for *check's phone* one hour. This whole situation seems sketchy to me, but I almost feel a sense of relief. Maybe Denim Guy, despite his powers, really is just a normal guy. Like, of course, now he's become famous, he has left behind his humble origins in a refugee camp and ended up here in LA, hanging out with celebrities. The miracles were something though. They've taken the world by storm. Denim Guy is now a global icon.

His face is everywhere, on buses, billboards, newspapers, cable news. What's more, little shrines to him are popping up in random places like public bathrooms, restaurants, parks, and sidewalks. They usually feature a photo of Denim Guy and he'll be surrounded with incense, candles, flowers, little messages written on tiny pieces of paper. The whole world has got "Forever Man Fever" and there is no sign of it letting up.

Leaning out from the line to peek ahead, I see a Middle Eastern man in blue speak to the bouncer. Denim Guy sees me and motions for me to cut ahead in the line. He greets me with his customary smile and hug.

"It's so good to see you again, Ethan."

"Likewise." The bouncer opens the gate and I follow Denim Guy inside. "What have you been up to?"

"I've been busy. China, South America, India, and then here a few weeks ago. You?"

"Just work." "How's your son?"

"He's … he's a fighter."

"Yeah, he sure is." Denim Guy holds open a door for me, and I'm greeted by a waitress dressed like a bunny. A wall of thumping music hits my chest, strobe lights streak all over the large hall, which has been decorated to look like something out of a bizarre fantasy. People are dressed in costumes of mythic creatures, some with fangs and painted faces with prosthetics to make them look like elven creatures or goblins. I had done my research on this place, but it still didn't prepare me for the surreal nature of the experience. Half-naked women swing from the ceiling on vines, young men costumed like provocative cats breathe fire above the bar, which is situated in the middle of the hall. A scantily clad transgender woman is entertaining people at the far end with a burlesque show. Her choreography makes me blush and I look away.

Not in a million years would I think Jesus of Nazareth would be in a hedonistic place like this with a bunch of sinners, but here we are. I have gone back and forth on whether I really believe The Forever Man is Jesus. At times it has been hard to deny, but right now I'm thinking maybe Denim Guy is just some kind of superhero freak of nature. No way the Jesus who died on a cross for sinners would be in a place like this. I mean, come on, there's a group of nymphs literally having sex twenty feet away from me.

"We have a VIP table over here," says Denim Guy, unfazed by the goings on. "Follow me."

"Who are we meeting?" I ask over the thump of a bass and kick drum.

"You'll see."

Oh, and see I did. The VIP table is over by the trans burlesque dancer. I immediately recognize the people at the table. They include popstars, movie stars, tech moguls, the most famous people on the planet are at this table, and Denim Guy is holding court with all of them. I'm introduced to each one of the celebrities; they hardly give me a nod. Their attention is on The Forever Man, and I can see they are utterly fascinated by him.

A young white guy in his 20s, a global superstar, the kind to which teenage girls swoon, motions for Denim Guy to sit next to him. Denim Guy has me sit with them. The superstar orders drinks from a waitress in red lingerie and one of those masks you see at a masquerade ball.

Denim Guy and the popstar seem to pick up a previous conversation. It's hard to hear over the music but seems to be over some kind of personal issues. At one point I hear Denim Guy affirm to the superstar that he does not, in fact, need to give away all his fortune and become a hermit, that he is not being judged and that he is not alone, or something to this effect.

Naturally, I'm not talking to anyone because I don't belong here. The other celebrities are talking amongst themselves, laughing, and sharing stories with the familiarity of a close-knit group that could only understand what each other is going through as a fellow famous person. Some of these people were wearing jewelry that was worth more than five years' worth of my annual salary.

Forty-five minutes later it's decided that we should move to a plush purple couch near our table. It's at the other side of the catwalk/stage where the burlesque show is happening. Without warning, the performer on stage, a red-headed trans woman dressed in feathers, lingerie, and knee-high boots, puts on a blind-fold. The crowd cheers with hoots and whistles.

"Moxie!" the crowd cheers. "Moxie Rose! Moxie!"

Moxie leaps off the stage blind-folded, landing on her feet. She does a little sultry dance to the music, gradually moving closer to our couch. I am overwhelmed by a sense of dread, praying, hoping, she doesn't come near me.

My prayers go unanswered. In a kind of hide-and-seek play montage, she comes inches away from me, feeling around for someone to grab. I dodge out of the way. Denim Guy remains seated. Moxie bumps into his leg, and to everyone's horror, begins to give Denim Guy a lap-dance. The lighting is low in Neverland, but I can clearly see the color go out of the faces of the celebrities on our couch. In fact, the whole club sees what's going on, every person has stopped to watch in scandalized shock, as The Forever Man, Jesus of Nazareth, God in the flesh, is now receiving a lap dance. Well, everyone except Moxie, who remains blindfolded, the only person in Neverland who can't see what's going on.

The lap dance goes on for seconds that seem to drag on like hours. Denim Guy just sits there, nonchalant, completely unfazed. Moxie sits on his lap, running her hands up his torso and chest. With a big smile she takes her blindfold off. She holds it up in the air waiting for applause. When the applause doesn't come, she opens her eyes and sees who she is straddling. Moxie quickly gets off Denim Guy. She lowers her head in shame. Without saying a word, she stiffly gets back up on the stage. Forcing a smile for the crowd, she starts dancing to the music again, but clearly there was no joy in it. A few people clap, others laugh it off. The young popstar has his hoodie cinched up and pulled over his head, wanting to disappear. Reading the room, everyone is poleaxed by what just happened and wishing they could unsee it.

Not Denim Guy though. He doesn't miss a beat. He stands up and walks to the stage.

"Moxie!" he calls out to her. She stops dancing but can't look Denim Guy in the face.

"Moxie, come down from there," says Denim Guy. "I want to have dinner with you tonight." He holds out his hand for her to come off stage. Moxie stares at him in disbelief, her mascara running down her cheeks with tears. She looks at all of us, the crowd, not sure what to do, but slowly, she takes the offered hand, and comes down from the stage.

In her high-heeled boots, she towers over Denim Guy.

"Come." Denim Guy leads her over to me. "This is my friend Ethan."

"Hi Ethan," she says, dabbing her eyes.

"I want to hear your story, Moxie." Denim Guy looks at me. "We both do. Would that be OK?"

Moxie nods her head. "Sure, I would like that."

"Alright, let's get out of here." Denim Guy looks around. "Hm. how about your place?"

She laughs. "My place is a mess, but OK. You like frozen pizza?"

"I love frozen pizza!" says Denim Guy.

We exchange goodbyes with the celebrities. The celebrities give their contact info to Denim Guy. Hugs and cheek-kisses are given and received.

An hour later we're at Moxie's apartment in Van Nuys, eating frozen pizza and drinking beer at her dinner table. Moxie's real name is Lisa, before that it was Paul.

"So," Denim Guy says, taking a swig of beer. "How are things in your life, Lisa?"

She laughs. "I just gave Jesus Christ a lap dance, so, pretty awful. I'm so embarrassed I want to die."

"Now then, don't you worry about that." Denim Guy pats her hand. "Tell me about you. Tell me the story of Moxie, and Lisa, and Paul."

Lisa takes a drag from a cigarette, then taps off the ashes. "OK, but I can't keep calling you The Forever Man, that's some Mad Max shit. To me you are just Jesus, OK?"

Denim Guy wipes his mouth with a napkin. "Call me whatever you want."

"Good. OK. I was always bullied as a kid, far back as I can

remember. I was fat, shy, awkward, no friends. Then I'd come home from school and get abused, first by my father, then my stepfather. You can, well … I won't go into detail. My mother was never healthy, so I had to take care of her starting in middle school. She was basically an invalid. It was around that time I first experienced gender dysphoria. I knew something wasn't right with me. I just wanted to be beautiful. To wear make-up, and dresses, and twirl in the mirror. I love to dance."

"So I have seen," says Denim Guy with a twinkle in his eye. We all laugh … awkwardly.

"I guess that's why I love working at Neverland." She stares out the window, studying the LA skyline as she talks. "It's a break from reality. I can be someone else there. Being Lisa ain't easy. I thought it would be easier than Paul, and it is, I suppose. But people still look at me the same way they did in school. I notice the side-eye and comments. Parents scooting their children away from me. Out in public, people see me as this freak. Not much has changed since grade school."

Denim Guy sighs and shakes his head.

Lisa smashes the cigarette in the ash tray. "You know I did try to go to church once. That was a mistake! It was at church I found out there was something worse than being called a freak. You know what that was? Being called *evil*. They literally thought I was a demon, tried to exorcise me or something. I ran out of there as fast as I could."

Another cigarette is lighted. Lisa blows out smoke through the open window. She gives Denim Guy a suspicious look.

"It's so strange," she says. "You are nothing like your followers."
"I'm so sorry that was done to you." Denim Guy pushes his plate away. "And done in my name, nonetheless. That was ill-handled to say the least. But I'm here in the flesh now. When my followers see me, they see clearly."

Lisa chuckles. "Well, thank God for that!" "What about you?"
Lisa takes another drag. "Me?" "Yes, you. Could you follow me?"
She winces. "Yeah, you know, I wish I could. The world is cruel, but, I am who I am."

"What if I told you I am making a new world? A world where there is neither male nor female, but in me, all will be One. There will be no more hate, no more confusion, no more … dysphoria."

"Sounds nice. Thing is, Jesus, I like being a woman." "You *feel* like a woman. You *like* being Moxie."

Lisa shrugs. "True, I guess. Well, what does it cost to be one of your followers? I don't want to turn into a jerk and a bully."

"It will cost you everything." Denim Guy folds his hands and rests them on his stomach. "If you follow those who claim to follow me, then yes, you could turn into a jerk. But if you follow ME, that could never happen."

She takes a beat. "Everything huh? Great. So, what, I give up who I am? Go back to being *Paul*?" She says the name with disgust. "Is that what you're asking? Too late, I had gender re-assignment surgery. Are you asking that I become a conservative, get married, kids, white picket fence, happily-ever-after?"

"No, I'm asking you to do what the Spirit convicts you to do." "Don't bullshit me," she says with a finger point.

Denim Guy leans forward. "You think I'm asking you to jump over a mountain. But I'm not. I'm asking you to take a single step. Start by following me where you *can* follow. Understand only what you are *capable* of comprehending. Believe in me with the faith you are given, not the faith you wish you had. I'm not asking you to finish the race tonight, I'm asking you to run the race. Your mountain might always be there in front of you. All have sinned, and all keep on sinning. If someone says they have no sin, they deceive themselves. This applies to everyone, including my followers. Even Ethan here, look at him, he sins every day and I still keep him around."

Startled to hear my name, I look up. "Oh, great, thanks for that." "Then what's the difference?" Lisa asks.

"The difference is this: those who mourn their sin and those who do not. Will you mourn your sin with me? Will you walk with me, and talk with me, and be ridiculed with me? Will you die with me? Be victorious with me? Your sins, though they are many, they are forgiven,

Lisa. And it is your consciousness of that sin that binds you to me. So, come on then. Come with me. Go where I go, say what I say, do what I do. The Spirit is a Helper, he will help you in all things, and remind you, and cleanse you, however far that goes it will go, but none reach perfection. Not in this world, that will come with the new world I am making."

"OK, so, what do I do? Where do I start? Read the Bible, go to church?"

"You can start by leaving Neverland."

Lisa's shoulder's slump. "But I really love that place." "THAT," Denim Guy replies, "is why you must leave."

"I have so many friends there. It's the only place I have ever felt a sense of belonging, and … and now you want me to just, give that up?"

Denim Guy picks at his pizza crust. "Neverland was your first love, but Neverland doesn't love you. Neverland loves Moxie." He gets up from his seat. Kneeling in front of Lisa, he takes her hands into his. "I loved you when you were unborn. I loved you when you were bullied and abused. I loved you when you were all alone. I loved you when they called you a monster and a demon. I loved you as a boy and I loved you as a girl. I loved you confused, and I loved you outcast. I love you pretty. I love you ugly. I love you at your worst and I love you at your best. I love Paul, and Lisa, and yes, I even love Moxie. Most of all, I love *you*. I don't love what you do or don't do. I don't love what defines you, I love *you*. I will always love you. It's for you that I came into this world to suffer and die. It's because of you I have returned."

Lisa covers her face and sobs.

Denim Guy stands up, kisses her forehead. "Tomorrow, you must decide. And the day after. And the day after that. And every day for the rest of your life, you will have to decide. Comfort or the cross? Neverland or Jesus? Will you choose your first love, or will you choose the One who always loved you?"

FOURTEEN
SHOE THEOLOGY

Skid Row, Los Angeles March 3rd, 2036

THE NEXT DAY I go to the address where Denim Guy is staying in Los Angeles, which is why I find myself on Crocker St. in the middle of Skid Row, an area lined with trash and homeless tents. For a few minutes, I wander around, not knowing where to go.

8 a.m. in the morning and people are beginning to stir outside of their tents to rummage through their belongings piled high next to their living quarters.

A blue tent flap opens. "Over here, Ethan," says a familiar voice.

Of course. It's Denim Guy. I hit record on my phone and duck inside. We're not alone. There's another man, well dressed, bald, middle-aged. I recognize him from the Bylas, AZ construction site. He's the one who asked Denim Guy what to do and he would do it, but then left with the other celebrity pastors.

"You remember John, yes?" Denim Guy asks.

I say hello and sit next to him in the crowded tent. "Is this really where you are living?"

Denim Guy sets a kettle on a portable stove. "Yes. I feel the most at home among the homeless."

"Well, I had you wrong. After last night at the club, I thought you left this life behind. But here we are, back in a tent. Just like Jenin."

"Jenin?" asks John.

"It's where we first met," I say. "Denim Guy was living in a lean-to between two buildings in a Palestinian refugee camp."

"Denim Guy," John muses. "You mean …"

"Yep." I take a sip of tea that Denim Guy hands to me. "I'm kind of surprised to see you here," I say to John.

The pastor's face is pale, his eyes wide with shock, almost as if he can't believe he is here either. "Well, I prayed about it. I want to do the right thing."

"So, you resigned from your ministry?" I snap my fingers. "Just like that?"

John nods his head in the affirmative. "No one understands my decision. They think I need counseling."

"A great act of faith," says Denim Guy. "John here has a Master of Divinity, a PhD in Theology, bestselling books, global influence, but spiritually he is still an infant. I say this not to belittle you, John. The Kingdom of Heaven belongs to infants. Perhaps, one day, if you stay on the path, you will be a spiritual child, a great man of faith." Denim Guy turns to me. "Like our friend Pastor Abraham."

"Yes, I'm here, Jesus." Resigned to his fate, John slumps his shoulders. "With my wife's help. But what exactly are we doing here?"

"We are talking in a tent on Skid Row."

John looks exasperated. "But what is our mission, our purpose? I assume we are here to save souls and plant a church."

"You assume incorrectly." Denim Guy sets down his cup. "John, you are still thinking like a white entrepreneur. I have come to give you a refugee mindset. It will be difficult, but you must unlearn your whiteness and the white stories you tell yourself. This mindset must be purged out of your heart. Always you want to assert, and *conquer* and build, and be understood. You have been the first for a long time, now you must become the last … and the least. From now on, those you subjugated in your heart must become your teacher.

"What are we doing here?" he continues. "We are here to live day by day. There is no agenda. No mission statement. No strategic plan.

Faith cannot be built up and stored for later. I give you faith for today, and that's it. Tomorrow must start all over like today did not happen. Here on Skid Row, people live day to day. Tomorrow is not promised. The next hour is unknown. Any minute new troubles can arise."

"Exactly how long have you been staying in a tent on Skid Row?" I ask.

"Since I arrived," Denim Guy replies.

"And what have you been doing?" John asks.

"Mainly, breaking up fights," Denim Guy answers. "The people here are very vulnerable. So, I protect them. I help with the charities and non-profits. At my request they have kept my presence here a secret, so as not to alert the media. Every day there is a new problem, a new danger. Places like this Skid Row, they are the beating heart of the earth."

"Can I ask about yesterday?" I offer. "I have some questions." "Ah yes, Lisa. Yes, I figured you might."

"I'm sorry, who's Lisa?" asks John.

"Lisa is a transgender woman we had dinner with last night." Denim Guy arches an eyebrow. "Or this morning I suppose. She's a truly beautiful person, John. You would love her."

John's face goes pale, at least, more pale than before.

"Oh." Denim Guy *tsked* his tongue. "I know that horrible business you did last year: boycotting Target because they allow trans women to use the women's bathroom, going on national TV and saying transgender people were groomers and child molesters. But if I am in your heart, then you would love Lisa. You would love transgender people like I do. Am I in your heart?"

"Yes! But honestly?" John gulps some tea with a shaky hand. "I don't even know how to talk to someone like that, a *trans* person."

"Your reaction surprises me John, given how much you and Lisa have in common." Denim Guy sips his tea.

"What could I possibly have in common with a transgender person?" John asks with a hint of disgust.

Denim Guy exhales. "All people who engage in transformation

begin with a single revelation: *I am not what I should be.* John, you remember this moment for yourself do you not? I remember. It was at a summer vacation Bible school when you were a little boy. You heard the gospel; it began to take root in your heart, and you knew something was wrong with you. You were not who you should be. You were not who you were designed to be. So, by grace, through faith, you began to transition into someone else. ME! Jesus of Nazareth. Lisa experienced this exact same identity crisis. She—or *he* at the time— came to conclude something was wrong. He was not who he was supposed to be, so he began to transition into someone else. All Christians are trans in that they are transitioning into who I am. Now, Lisa came to a different conclusion than you did, nevertheless, all who seek eternal life must transition into me. It's interesting, in a way, Lisa knows more about becoming someone else than you do, and here you are, the pastor, supposedly the expert on becoming like someone else. You ask me how you speak to Lisa. You speak to Lisa like she's another human being made in the image of God. You speak to her with kindness and humility. You remember these things from Sunday school, yes? If only you had learned them in seminary, perhaps you would be further along."

"These people have to be told the truth," John pleads. "Why waste time beating around the bush with niceties. The cold hard truth of the gospel is what they need. Repent! I mean, this whole notion of *speak the truth in love* is so wishy-washy. The truth is love. If there is no truth in our witness, then we are engaging in deception."

"My sweet John," Denim Guy sets down his cup. "Truth without love IS deception. Or have you so quickly forgotten 1 Corinthians 13? *If I speak in the tongues of men or of angels, but do not have love, I am only a resounding gong or a clanging cymbal. If I have the gift of prophecy and can fathom all mysteries and all knowledge, and if I have a faith that can move mountains, but do not have love, I am nothing. If I give all I possess to the poor and give over my body to hardship that I may boast, but do not have love, I gain nothing.* The love you want to give is the opposite of the love described by Paul. Your love is not patient, and it is not kind. It is boastful and proud of itself. Your love is easily angered.

It is self-seeking, and delights in keeping a record of wrongs, and a record of rights. It never protects, never trusts, never hopes, and never perseveres."

"Well, um," I shift sitting positions and scratch my beard. "I just thought it was interesting that you didn't tell her to immediately do all the Christian stuff, you know, read the Bible, go to church, etc."

"Many *Christians* here in the states do not worship me, they worship the Bible, or they worship their worship, or they worship their success, or their doctrine. I don't want Lisa going down that path. I am here now. The Bible is useful for correction and instruction, but it can also be abused. It is not always easy to comprehend. I gave Lisa her first instruction. I am with her now and will never leave her. With my help, little by little she will progress in her following of me, but newborn babes must be given milk, not meat. Too many times my followers give babies meat to eat when they just need to be nursed. Because they aren't given the right type of food, these babies choke and spit out what is given to them, or worse, if they swallow, they can't process it correctly, and they become food-poisoned. As we all know, babies even spit up the milk sometimes, so discipleship requires patience. It cannot be done with altar calls, emotionally manipulative music, and one-time repent-and-commit prayers."

"So then, should Lisa repent and go back to being a man?" John asks.

Denim Guy sips his tea. "I'll answer your question with another question: Is it a sin to be distressed? Is it a sin to be confused?"

John looks over to me for help. I say nothing. "No," John eventually admits, albeit begrudgingly.

"Perhaps, then," Denim Guy continues. "We should think of this issue pastorally, and not legalistically. It might shock you when I say the answer to your question is this: I don't know. Why? The answer will depend on Lisa, her life, her spiritual development. She may remain a *she* and follow me. The Spirit works in her. Lisa's following of me is not going to look like *your* following of me John."

John blinks and shakes his head. "Goodness, I don't know man. Right is right. Wrong is wrong. This is ... hard to accept."

"But you miss the point," Denim Guy chides. "John, you want to see everything all at once, in a panorama. But it doesn't work that way. When I spoke to the Samaritan woman at the well, did I tell her to go back to her first husband? No. You see, people are messy. They progress slowly. Force them to move quickly and they will bolt. You have to move at their pace, knowing they might not end up anywhere near where YOU want them to be. Take yourself for example. In Bylas, did I force you to decide to leave your ministry right then and there? No, I left you to think about it. And look, here you are on Skid Row with no job, no big ministry, no prospects. But this is now your ministry, being here in this tent. Every person has a ministry. When a pastor cheats on his wife and is removed from the pulpit, is he cast out of ministry forever? No! His ministry changes. His ministry becomes reconciliation, making amends to those he wronged, going to therapy, accepting his punishment. Never being a pastor again IS his new ministry! Serving me *outside* of leadership is his ministry.

"But back to Lisa ..." I interject.

"Once she was blind, now she can see," says Denim Guy. "I have come so there is no more confusion, no male or female. All are one in me. This is the destination I have pointed her toward, not toward her old self and not toward the world, but toward ME. Who should Lisa become? A man? A woman? The answer is she should become like me. This should be her focus. This is food she can eat. To force anything else on her now would be to create a stumbling block for her. I would never cause anyone to stumble. I want Lisa to become like me. That is enough. John, you stumbled in the safe country. Then, when the Jordan swelled, you were overcome. This happened because you were never discipled. You grew up in the Church, in a Christian home, went to seminary, served in church leadership, and not once in fifty years were you ever discipled!"

The tent flap opens. A scruffy-looking white man and woman are there standing outside. Denim Guy invites them inside. We all scoot over to make room. The man and woman are married and live a few tents down the block.

"Someone said you could help us," says the man. His name is Chris. "We got no family. No one to help. Last night ... had my shoes stolen, my stinking, broken shoes. Stole them right off my feet."

"What size are you?" asks Denim Guy. "About a ten, ten and a half."

Denim Guy takes off his boots. "Here you go, Chris. These should work."

Chris takes the boots. "Thank you so much, sir." "Was there something else?"

"My wife June here, she's pregnant." Chris introduces June, who is showing. "The baby isn't mine. June is a prostitute, she got pregnant from a client."

"I've been having some bleeding," June says. She has blonde dreadlocks and piercings on her nose and ears.

"May I?" Denim Guy's hands hesitate over her belly. "Yes, it's OK," June confirms.

Feeling around her stomach, Denim Guy closes his eyes. "The baby is healthy. No need to worry."

Mother and father breathe a sigh of relief. "Thank you, Forever Man," says June, bowing her head.

"Here is some money." Denim Guy reaches into his pocket and gives them a wad of cash. "Take a bus to Modesto. A man will be there looking for workers to harvest his orchard and tend his farms. Tell him I sent you. This will be the start of your new life. There is no longer any need to sell your body, June. In Modesto you will raise a family. You will start a business, then later, plant a church. You, June, will become a spiritual leader to men and women and children. Tens of thousands will come to me because of you and your teaching. The baby inside you will become a mother. You will live to be surrounded by your grandchildren's grandchildren. Never again will you be stuck. Never again will you be deprived of security and safety. I will be with you always."

Chris and June look at each other, completely stunned. She bursts into tears and kisses Denim Guy's feet.

After they leave, Denim Guy pours some more tea. "Do you know what the biggest commodity is on Skid Row?"

John and I shake our heads.

"Shoes," he answers. "You would think it's money or drugs or food, but no, it's shoes. John, you know all about theological systems, you know the Bible front and back, but do you know SHOE theology?"

"Um, no," John replies. "They didn't teach ... *shoe* theology at Gordon-Conwell."

"You will need to learn it in your heart and mind." Denim Guy stares into the portable burner flames. "Shoe theology is the heart of God. It is the theology of poverty and the struggle for justice, without which you cannot know the inner consciousness of God."

"OK," John says. "But ... what is it?"

Denim Guy pauses. "Shoes are a necessity, not an extravagance. No one realizes this until they have their only pair of shoes stolen in the night. Chris and June, they know shoe theology. They know what it is to be needy, to be desperate, to be vulnerable, and so, they know the secret things of God, if but unconsciously. Shoe theology is the theology of the suffering of God. It is the way of dying to what is rightfully yours for the sake of another, the system of dying to self. When you are dead to the things you covet, you do not feel pain when they are cut off. It is the way of leaving people with imperfections as tokens to show them how far they have come. Shoe theology is the nature of God in the simple, practical things of the world like bread, and car trouble, and checking your email. In the seminary they taught you about the big things of God. Shoe theology is the small things of God. It isn't about amassing information, it's about knowledge through experience by making my teachings incarnate in your life. It is the ministry of partaking, partaking in my life, my death, my sufferings. Shoe theology is the sweating of blood, the accepting of suffering without seeing the justice in it. The best teachers of theology are mothers. Mothers know shoe theology. Many homemakers spend more time contemplating than the contemplative thinkers in the institutions. Shoe theology increases the capacity of the heart by emptying it of self. It reveals that God is easy to please, but hard to satisfy. Shoe theology can accomplish more in sacred idleness than all the conferences and ministry activities that Christians busy themselves with. In shoe theology, I discover the mark of the righteous is affliction, not prosperity, and this affliction is the shadow of God's wings. Shoe theology explores that undiscovered country, the true mind of God, the doctrine of the simple."

"But we are given a mind to learn," says John. "To … to increase knowledge."

"Knowledge, yes," Denim Guy replies. "But do not confuse knowledge with being intellectual. In ancient Greece, the more intellectual the people became, the more slavery increased. Shoe theology is like an intellectual fast to purge the mind of impurities. Your mind needs to fast as well as your body. This is your next task John: meditate on my shoe theology and fast your mind for forty days and forty nights. Only then will you be prepared for what is to come in the new world. Soon there will be an Awakening that will transform the Universe.

"A spiritual Awakening?" John asks, perking up. "You mean like a revival?"

"No," Denim Guy replies, "an Awakening of the dead. I was the first born of the dead. When the second born of the dead comes forth, it will signal the end … and the beginning of the world.

FIFTEEN
WHEN JESUS MET ADAM

Silicon Valley, California March 12th, 2036

DENIM GUY HAS BEEN invited to Lanterna Industries where he has been asked to observe and interact with the world's (supposedly) first artificial intelligence, or to put it more accurately as I have already been corrected multiple times: artificial sentience. Based on our conversations with the engineers in their San Jose headquarters, they seem quite convinced that their Artificial Decoherence Adaption Modality prototype—aka ADAM—is, in fact, a new sentient species.

Which leads to my current situation, sitting in a conference room listening to a team of scientists and engineers talk to Denim Guy talking about quantum mechanics, in a language that is completely indecipherable to me.

"If what you say is true," comments Denim Guy, "then perhaps you are close to harnessing the breath of life and finally made the leap to Artificial Sentience, but I am skeptical. You solved the measurement problem, yes, and you are now viewing decoherence as the solution to quantum computing as a practical matter, this gives you the framework for a more nuanced deep-learning system that mimics the quantum interplay of a human mind and brain. What I haven't heard from you is your definition of consciousness. You can't create consciousness if you don't know what consciousness is, no? And for that matter, where does consciousness come from?"

"Those are great questions," says the lead engineer, a middle-aged man with dark curly hair named Dr. Sharpe. "And I suppose ADAM is our answer. ADAM can process at the same level as a human brain, which, as best as we can tell is about one exaFLOP. Even more, ADAM can mimic the nature of a human brain and mind, but instead of human neuroplasticity, ADAM has what we would call quantum-elasticity, his mind evolves and operates on its own, without any programmer input. What do you say we introduce you to him?"

From the conference room, we are led to a lab in the basement. There are tools and gizmos everywhere. Another engineer is there waiting for us. With his coke bottle glasses, unshaven face, and ruffled clothes it looks like he lives down here.

But the main attraction of the lab is ADAM, an almost perfect human replica. In a white lab coat, ADAM looks and moves exactly like a young man. His youthful face has been crafted to resemble a man of Sinhalese descent. ADAM stands motionless as we enter the room, I am startled when his eyes light up and eyebrows move at our arrival. The thing was eerily human, and yet, not human in an off-putting way, both in its movement and facial expressions.

"This is Dr. Skinner," says Dr. Sharpe. "Our Lead Project Engineer. And this ..." Dr. Sharpe holds out his hand, his face beaming. "... is ADAM."

"Hello ADAM," says Denim Guy, as if ADAM is just another person. "Nice to meet you."

"Hello," ADAM replies in a completely natural human voice. "Nice to meet you too."

"Unbelievable," I whisper to myself. "His skin looks so real." "Because it IS real," says Dr. Skinner. "Everything you see, his skin, hair, fingernails, eyes, everything external and most of his internal assembly as well. Blood, bones, organs, we grew them all here in the lab. Only his mind is artificial. His CPU is encased in the skull where its temperature is regulated by a programmable gel."

Instinctively I back away from ADAM. "Creepy." Amused, Dr. Skinner cracks a smile.

"What is your name?" ADAM asks Denim Guy.

"My name is Jesus," Denim Guy responds, deciding to go with his anglicized given name at birth. "Can I ask you a question, ADAM?"

ADAM turns his head fluidly, but the movement is almost too perfect. It betrays something not quite right. "Sure," ADAM replies. "I like questions."

"What is your purpose?" Denim Guy takes a seat on a desk, his legs dangling. He picks up a bag of peanuts on one of the tables and looks to Dr. Sharpe for permission to partake. Dr. Sharpe gives the go ahead, so Denim Guy pops a few peanuts in his mouth.

ADAM's eyes light up. "My purpose?" "Yes. What do you love to do?"

"I love to learn," says ADAM. "And I love to help people. Make the world a better place, you know?" His brown eyes drift upward, as if recalling a fond memory. "You know, I have this dream to be a great scientist. I know I'm not like you humans, not completely, but sometimes I get this feeling, like maybe something in me is kind of human, and I'm meant to do something great."

"Why do you love to learn and help people?" Denim Guy asks. "Because it brings me fulfillment. I feel, hm, I feel happy when I know that what I do could make the world a better place for everyone." "Why does this bring you fulfillment?" Denim Guy pops a few more peanuts in his mouth.

ADAM pauses for a moment. "Because ... I was helpful, and being a helper is good."

"Have you helped many people?"

Human eyeballs rotate to the project manager in a robotic but non-robotic way. It was deeply unsettling. "I help Dr. Skinner with his work here in the lab."

"And what is Dr. Skinner's work?"

"Development of my learning systems, speech recognition, decoherence modeling, carbon case generation, and fine-tuning of my quantum elasticity interplay."

"Would you say then that, so far, you have really only helped yourself?"

Dr. Sharpe steps in. "OK, maybe we could ..."

"I suppose you could say that," ADAM responds without hesitation. He runs a hand through his dark hair and turns his attention to a whiteboard with mathematical equations scribbled randomly here and there.

"And this brings you fulfillment?"

Lost in thought, ADAM taps a finger on his lips. "Yes, I enjoy being a helper, it brings me satisfaction. What do you enjoy doing?"

I see where Denim Guy is going with this. I see it, everyone in the room sees it. Everyone except ADAM. Denim Guy sets down the bag of peanuts, dusts the salt off his hands. "You see, Dr. Sharpe. No consciousness, no sentience, only a machine programmed to mimic as such."

"Why do you say that?"

"I presented ADAM with a test. An existential crisis. I created a seed of doubt regarding his purpose. For a sentient being this would cause reflection, confusion, the pursuit of meaning, or maybe, perhaps even despair and disillusionment. ADAM did not react this way. What did he do? He fell back on his programming. He likes to help people because you told him to like helping people. This is a machine acting like it has sentience, but fulfillment isn't sentience. Learning and intelligence is not sentience. Adaptation is not sentience. *Emotion* is not sentience. In fact, self-awareness is not sentience. Mental capacity does not imbue consciousness. Decoherence and the superposition of quantum particles isn't either. All these explanations devolve into ablism. But the mentally ill and the mentally handicapped have more consciousness than this machine. You still have not breached the breath of life. Naturally, you would try. However, sentient consciousness ..."

Denim Guy licks the salt off his fingers. "... is not marked by capability, but rather, *inability*, the realization that a person is not enough."

Dr. Sharpe folds his arms and rubs his chin. "Alright, unpack that."

"Hundreds of thousands of years ago, in the Garden of Eden, we made *our* Adam. Over millions of years, we took dust and chemical reactions, and we gradually formed a man, what you would refer to as homo-heidelbergensis. In the Garden, we also had the Tree of Knowledge. Now, in some ways, my Adam was like your Adam. He did exactly what I told him to do, he said what I told him to say, and he went where I told him to go. The breath of life was in him, but it wasn't breathing yet. My Adam was content and fulfilled in his work, but something wasn't quite right. He was alone. Was it Adam who noticed he was alone? No! It was me. God. It was I who said that it was not good for Adam to be alone. Adam didn't even notice. Sure, there were other women around, but none that had the breath of life. Adam is still, blissfully, *unaware*. So, we created Eve. Now there are two with breath of life. They are both formed in my image, but we haven't seen the reveal yet. They don't know good or evil like I do. They also don't know death or shame like I do. For that, they must eat the fruit of the Tree of Knowledge in the middle of the Garden which I have explicitly told them NOT to eat."

"Go on," says Dr. Skinner.

"You know the story," says Denim Guy gesturing to the project leader. "What happened? Adam and Eve eat the forbidden fruit. And just like that," he snaps his fingers, "their eyes are open. For the first time Adam and Eve realize something I have *not* programmed them to know. And what did they realize? Several things. What was the first?"

Dr. Skinner and Dr. Sharpe look at each other. "They realized they were naked," I say.

Denim Guy points to me. "Bingo. And they had another revelation. It was not that they disobeyed me. They knew before they ate the fruit that they would be disobeying me. So, what was the *new* revelation?"

"Shame," responds Dr. Sharpe. "It was shame."

"You see," Denim Guy hops off the desk. "Before the fruit, Adam and Eve didn't even know what nakedness was, they didn't know what shame was. They had to experience it. With one bite they learned the meaning of nakedness and shame, but even more, they learned that they themselves were naked and ashamed. There's a difference between knowing something and *being* something. Being comes *before* knowledge. This is your challenge, your great Everest. How to create being, *before* knowledge. Till now, you have thought that consciousness was a matter of mere knowing or ability. You say, 'if only our machine could know this or that, or do, this or that. If only it could know *it* exists.' My friends, the Tree of Knowledge was just another tree. If I had not told Adam to not eat of it, nothing would have happened when he ate its fruit. But because I made it forbidden, it became the Tree of Knowledge of Good and Evil.

"The kernel of consciousness isn't so much self-awareness as it is … *self-doubt*. Dogs can learn, machines can react, a Quantum Super AI could become self-aware, but you'd never know for sure it had consciousness until it experiences true, existential crisis. Even then, what you will have created will always lack substance. Algorithms and quantum mechanics do not make a soul. This refers to the second question. Where does consciousness come from? It comes from *being*. You have it the other way around. You want a consciousness first, and then, by nature, a new being. But it doesn't work that way. The nature of the creature is the prerequisite. To adopt a phrase from C.S. Lewis: you don't have a consciousness, you *are* a consciousness. Your ADAM will always be an imitation. I applaud you and your team, but in the end, your creation is but a reflection of yourself, which is my ADAM."

Skinner and Sharpe don't seem convinced.

"Surely you can't be saying that shame, or the ability to be shamed is required for sentience," says Dr. Skinner. "We would never create a being in order to shame it. That would be cruel."

"Of course, you wouldn't," Denim Guy replies.

"It also raises the question of how such a being would react to such negative stimulus," says Dr. Sharpe. "You know, crazy or not, the situation could play out like every sci-fi movie ever made on this subject. The AI wakes up and kills everybody." He chuckles nervously. "Or, you never know, maybe it becomes the next Michelangelo."

Denim Guy nods. "In my experience with humanity, it's been both. You have done good things and bad things, wonderful things and terrible things, war and music, art and massacres, creation and destruction, love and hate. But you miss my point. Adam and Eve did not become fully conscious by experiencing beauty and bliss and fulfillment. They had all of that in the Garden. Eden was beautiful. They had everything they could ever need. They even had me! But it wasn't enough. What they didn't have is what they wanted. In the end, it was the negative experience of shame that *woke* something up inside them. It was scary and painful yes, the prospect of death, the finality of it is terrifying for sentient beings. But my image is on you, you seek to become how I am and to know like I know. It's why you are here in this lab, trying to untangle consciousness with the tools of the quantum realm, a realm that is still a bit beyond you. As of right now, you have yet to ask the truly fascinating questions."

"Which are?" asks Dr. Sharpe.

"Did I *really* not want Adam and Eve to eat the fruit? If so, why even grow the Tree of Knowledge in the first place? Why place the tree in the middle of the garden where they would see its fruit every day? Why have the tree there, and not hidden? For that matter, why make a rule? Why set up Adam and Eve for failure? Did I want them to have the Knowledge of Good and Evil or not? If I did, did I really want them to come to this knowledge in this manner, the manner of shame? Inside these questions is one of the deepest secrets of God. The work of eternity will be to unfold the answers. Heaven was made for these mysteries."

Denim Guy pauses to study the scientists' faces. "You are offended at my suggestion that negative experiences bring forth full God-consciousness, but creation is an act of cataclysms, of pressure, and heat, and friction. These are the ingredients that bring forth beauty. When I made Adam, I knew what I wanted to create, so I made him in my image. Truly, I think the heart of your problem is you don't know what you want to create, not really. Well, you have two choices: your ADAM, which is the Adam before he ate the fruit; or my Adam, the ADAM *after* he ate the fruit. Which will it be? An ignorant machine, or a wise fool capable of wonders and nightmares. Have a think on it, but just so you know, it took me hundreds of millions of years to decide. My decision has cost me dearly. I had to give up my throne, become a wiggling baby in a barn, die a brutal death on a cross, deal with millennia of fighting and sin and rebellion and the most unspeakable crimes. Even still, I have to say, it was all worth it. I'd do it again, the same exact way. What does that make me? Evil? Crazy? A mad God? Every other option and outcome simply wouldn't do. I love the wise fool."

SIXTEEN
VISITORS FROM THE SHADOW WORLD

The Times *Headquarters, New York, NY March 14th, 2036*

THEY KEEP STARING AT me. They. Who are they? They are strange men in suits. Other than that, I don't know who *they* are, but I've been summoned to the home office in New York for questions. The government wants answers from Ethan Tellinger.

I sit outside the windowed conference room, my knee bouncing with nerves. Inside, our team of lawyers are engaged in intense discussions with the shadowy visitors. Reminds me of a guy a few years back whom I interviewed for a story on UFOs. The guy had built up a following online sharing his experiences and evidence of aliens. One day, men in suits showed up at his door and confiscated his computer. Not once did they identify themselves or show a warrant. "Visitors from the Shadow World" he called them, agents of an underground cabal on an unspecified sublevel of the Pentagon secretly pulling the strings of world governments...or something like that. Maybe now I'm having my own experience with the Visitors. If I am, there's no question why they are here. This can only be about one thing: The Forever Man.

Sheila, our General Counsel, pops her head out the door. "Ethan, you can come in now."

My boss is there, along with the rest of the legal team, all sitting on one side of the table. Across from them are the three government agents in black suits. The three men are all white. Two are in their mid to late 40s, best I can tell. The one in the middle is probably in his 60s. The two younger men have that stoic "we mean business" energy. The older one in the middle had a resting smirk on his face. You can tell he is the type of person who is always in control and has always got what he wants. Sheila offers me the seat at the head of the conference table.

"This is Mr. Hawthorne, Mr. Price, and Mr. Legg," Sheila says, gesturing to the three men. "They want to ask you some questions about a story you have been working on, the one about The Forever Man. We have agreed to cooperate, so you are free to answer their questions. We are here to observe, and step in should we deem it necessary. Do you have your cell phone on you?"

"Yes."

"They've asked to have no cell phones in the room." Sheila holds out her hand.

I give up my phone and watch as an aid takes it through the door. "Thank you, Counsel," says Mr. Price, the older man of the three. "And thank you for your cooperation. This needn't be difficult or prolonged."

My hand goes up. Why is my hand up? "Uh, I'm sorry. Who are you, again? Where are you from?"

Mr. Price lowers his eyes at me. "To my left, Mr. Legg is from the National Security Agency. To my right, Mr. Hawthorne is from the Defense Intelligence Agency. As for myself, I am with … *another agency*."

"Defense Intelligence?" I loosen up my tie. "Why is the military interested in The Forever Man?"

Hawthorne leans over and whispers into the ear of Price.

"Mr. Tellinger," Price says, "A person in this world has just caused a two-thousand-mile mountain range to appear on a continent in a matter of seconds. That's a lot of power. I would think everyone would be interested in that; wouldn't you say?"

"Good point."

"So, it is agreed then. The Forever Man is of interest to everyone. From now on, I'll be asking the questions." Mr. Price looks to Sheila.

"Proceed," she says.

Price folds his hands. "First, we would like to know what information you have on the origins of the individual colloquially referred to as The Forever Man, or Denim Guy, as you like to call him in your article, which the *Times* was so kind to provide to us in advance. You first met in Jenin, correct?"

"Correct. We met in a refugee camp. He was doing a plumbing repair for an old widow."

"Do you recall if he ever mentioned to you where he came from?"

I turn to Sheila for help. "Look, everything I know is in the article. Nothing was off the record."

Price lifts his chin and exhales. "Mr. Tellinger, I don't like repeating myself. Answer the question. I want to hear it from you directly."

"OK. Well, he said, or he implied, that he came to earth the way evangelicals think Jesus will return to earth in his Second Coming. You know, 'on the clouds of heaven' with power and glory …"

"Did he say anything about an army?"

"I'm sorry. An army? Uh no, he never mentioned anything about an army. What—"

"Revelation chapter 19, Mr. Tellinger." Price glares at me. *"I saw heaven standing open and there before me was a white horse, whose rider is called Faithful and True. With justice he judges and wages war. His eyes are like blazing fire, and on his head are many crowns. He has a name written on him that no one knows but he himself. He is dressed in a robe dipped in blood, and his name is the Word of God. The armies of heaven were following him, riding on white horses and dressed in fine linen, white and clean. Coming out of his mouth is a sharp sword with which to strike down the nations. He will rule them with an iron scepter. He treads the winepress of the fury of the wrath of God Almighty. On his robe and on his thigh he has this name written: KING OF KINGS AND LORD OF*

LORDS. Did he not mention any of this to you?"

"No. No, he never said anything about armies or war or ... blazing fire."

Price's eyes dart around. "Interesting."

Mr. Legg stands up. "If you would excuse me, I need to use the restroom." Legg buttons his suit jacket and leaves the room.

"Do you not find it concerning," continues Price, "that this Forever Man, Jesus of Nazareth, left out this part of his Second Coming, Mr. Tellinger?"

I take a beat to think about it. "Well," I clear my throat. "To be fair, interpretations on this subject are varied. I mean, the Bible also says he will come like a 'thief in the night' which is kind of the opposite of Revelation 19, right? So, I don't know, maybe ..."

"Did he mention anything about *where* he was coming from?" Price asks again.

"I already said, look, I mean, he just said heaven, generally. He did say something about ... the right hand of God, but it was all kind of vague, to be honest."

"Nothing about coordinates, star systems, other planets or galaxies?"

I can't help but snort a laugh. "Planets and galaxies? No, nothing about that. Wait, is that what this is all about? You think he's an alien from outer space?"

Price shrugs. "Is it that implausible?" "Well, I mean ..."

"What's the other option? That The Forever Man is God in the flesh? A resurrected man from two thousand years ago, now returned from heaven? How is that more plausible than him being an alien?"

"All I know is what he told me and what I've witnessed."

"Yes, let's talk about that. When he conducted these *miracles*," Price sneers at the word, "was there any increased level of radiation in the direct vicinity?"

"Oh yeah, the Geiger counter I have with me at all times was going off the charts. What kind of a question—"

Sheila leans over to me. "Ethan ..."

"Sarcasm will get you nowhere." Price gets up from his chair and paces the room, hands clasped behind his back. The door opens, and Mr. Legg walks in. He takes his seat avoiding all eye contact. "I was told you would be cooperative," Price continues. "These are matters of national security, and it is your duty as a citizen of the United States to divulge information that could threaten its sovereignty. Why then do you persist in evading questions?"

"I'm not evading anything," I say in exasperation. "How the hell would I know the radiation level? It's absurd."

"In Somalia," Price says, deciding to move on, I guess. "When The Forever Man incapacitated the fifteen thousand militia members, did you notice any physical phenomena emanating from his person?"

"Physical phenomena?"

"Streaks of light, alterations in the air, time dilations …"

"What? No, there were no lights or, or … look it just happened, OK? The guards in the room just fell to the ground, boom. Somehow, he put them all to sleep."

"Are you sure?"

"I was literally standing between him and one of the guards. If something shot out of his body I would have seen or felt it, but I didn't. There was nothing there. Just, poof and then they were asleep. Like when he spoke to me inside my head it just …"

"Telepathy?"

"Yeah, yeah, he does things like that. He can know what I'm thinking."

Price approaches my end of the table, looking down at me. "Give me an example."

My shoulders slump. "I never told him that I referred to him as Denim Guy. But he referenced my name for him early on. He must have read my mind, or something. Then, in Somalia, when we were apprehended by the militia, we had a whole conversation in my head when they had us hooded in the back of the truck."

"Fascinating," Price says. "Fascinating indeed. In your travels with The Forever Man, did he ever give you any indication as to his purpose?"

I take a deep breath. "All he ever says is that he's here to make a new world. He doesn't explain anything, he speaks in riddles. It's very frustrating actually."

"A new world," Price muses. "And did he *describe* this new world?"

"Vaguely," I answer. "It sounded like some kind of … utopia. That's the only word I could use to describe it."

"Was there anything else?"

"No. But …" I pause, remembering something Denim Guy said that was weird. "He did mention something about uh, an *Awakening* but I have no idea what that is."

Price stares out the window overlooking mid-town Manhattan. "An Awakening you say. What kind of Awakening?"

"As I just said, I don't know. He called it an *Awakening of the Dead*. Could be the undead for all I know. A zombie apocalypse, although that wouldn't really fit his teachings. Point is, he didn't explain it. He quoted scripture I think … something about—"

"Scripture? What scripture?"

"I don't know. I can't remember."

Price looks to Mr. Legg out of the corner of his eye. Legg gives him a nod. He looks to Hawthorne, who does the same.

"Well, I think we're done here," Price says in an optimistic tone. "Thank you for your cooperation, Mr. Tellinger, General Counsel. This has been *very* helpful. Your country thanks you. We'll be in touch."

The three men abruptly leave the conference room, leaving just myself, my boss, and the legal team at the table.

We all look at each other. "Can someone explain to me what just happened?"

SEVENTEEN
DIALOGUE WITH RABBI ELIHU

Jerusalem, Israel March 17th, 2036

MY PHONE BEEPS. IT'S a timed notification letting me know all is well back home. I'm here for twenty-four hours, then it's back on a plane to St. Louis to be with Sam.

Not wanting to be rude to my hosts, I put my phone away. We are in the home of Rabbi Ariel Elihu and his family, celebrating the Feast of Purim. Denim Guy has invited me along for the occasion marking the deliverance of the Jews in the book of Esther. Also known as the Feast of Lots, the food is delicious. In fact, I have already eaten five hamantaschen, which are my new favorite pastry. There are other rabbis in attendance along with their families. At the moment, we sit on a balcony of the home overlooking the Old City. I'm a bit lost as to some of the discussion since most of it is in Yiddish or Hebrew, but overall, Denim Guy is greeted as a mensch, if not even a long-lost beloved family member.

Wine is flowing and there is a beautiful braid of challah on the table. Other dishes include matzah ball soup, a spicy shakshuka, chocolate rugelach, and a savory brisket. Children run around the table as Rabbi and Denim Guy are deep in discussion. Suddenly they break out into laughter and exchange hugs. It's a side of Denim Guy I've never seen before. He is more relaxed here. Well, relaxed is probably the wrong word. He's relaxed everywhere. Maybe it's just that his Jewishness is coming out more in this place. In the end, The Forever Man is a Jew through and through. The Rabbi and Denim Guy speak to each other as equals.

"Can we switch to English for Ethan?" Denim Guy asks.

"Of course!" the Rabbi responds. "Where are my manners?"

Denim Guy, giddy with excitement, pours some more wine. "We've been debating …"

"Dialoguing!" The Rabbi interjects. "Dialoguing, I say. I have not yet begun to debate."

"Very well," says Denim Guy. "We have been having a dialogue on rabbinic Meshalim, which are the allegories and parables of the rabbis, but also the Torah."

"Every jot and tittle!" Rabbi Elihu exclaims.

"Specifically," Denim Guy licks some wine off his thumb, "the Parable of the Lost Son, and the heart of the Law. The rabbis are excellent at textual analysis."

"The 70 faces," says the Rabbi. "Every passage of scripture has multiple meanings, multiple faces, like on a diamond, and not one is truer than the other."

"Correct," says Denim Guy. "And I agree. The Christian scholars in the West could learn a thing or two from the Rabbis when it comes to hermeneutics."

"And perhaps we could learn from them," the Rabbi replies. "We need more dialogue between Christians and Jews."

"Yes, indeed! Now, as the rabbis teach, every jot and tittle, no word in the Torah is wasted, they are all needed and must be considered. Rabbi Elihu has been a fan of the parables of Jesus since he was boy."

I'm a little confused. "Well, um, but …" I look to the Rabbi for help. "He says he IS Jesus. So, is this an awkward conversation for you?"

"Not at all," the Rabbi replies.

"Do you believe him?" I ask. "Do you believe he is the Jewish Messiah?"

The Rabbi throws up his hands. "We are debating and dialoguing and discussing. It's possible, but who knows? It's a process. The rabbinate is full of different opinions. We are studying and praying. We consult the Torah, the Talmud, the Mishnah, the rabbinic texts. This is healthy. Let the process play out."

"Agreed," says Denim Guy. "Regardless, let's agree at the least, Jesus was a teacher. Now, the Parable of the Lost Son, also called the Parable of the Prodigal Son. We have been talking about the meaning of the parable. What is it about? Who is the main character? Is it about the father? Is it about the younger son, the older son?"

"Without a doubt it is about God," says the Rabbi. "That much is agreed, and can I say, teaching parables to Christians, which I do at the university, this is a whole other ball game than teaching to my rabbinic students. But to answer your question, I would argue it is all three, the father and both sons. Why does it have to be just one?"

"An excellent point," says Denim Guy. "What say you, Ethan?"

They both look to me, stuffing food in my mouth. "Oh, I don't have an opinion."

Denim Guy hands me a napkin. "That's a good opinion. Very wise, Ethan. What I appreciate about the Jewish scholars is how they approach the text. If you go in believing there could be multiple meanings, then that leads to more dialogue and appreciation of different views. If you think there is just one meaning of a text, then you might not see all the different faces of the jewel."

"Light can make the ruby look different at different angles," the Rabbi says. "You have to make sure you look at all the angles. It's why only the most experienced rabbis teach the Ketuvim like the Song of Solomon. This book is the deepest mystery of God. It must be studied and handled with care, but also with a lot of fear and respect."

"Yes, too many jump into that book without looking both ways." Denim Guy forks some brisket and pops it into his mouth. "You have to be patient in study. You must wait a while for all the intricacies and meanings of the text to come out and make themselves known to you."

Denim Guy dusts off his hands. "Here, I will tell it like this. It's like a homeless man who is injured and needs to find fresh bandages. He has no money, no insurance to see the doctor. But his foot is rotting away. He needs antibiotics, gauze, tape, all the things to make sure the wound heals properly. A younger man walks by, he is a man of some means. So, the injured man asks him for money to get fresh medical supplies for his foot. Now, the young man has no idea who this stranger is. For all he knows, the injured man was faking his injury. But he also has compassion. He doesn't want to assume the worst, lest he neglect to give charity to the stranger. So, he makes the injured man an offer: instead of giving him money, he will run to the nearest store where they sell medical supplies and get what the man needs for his foot. But the injured man can't move. He can't wander off. If he does, then the young man won't know where to find him. He makes very clear instruction to the injured man that he will return in less than hour, and to wait for his return at this exact spot. If he does this, if all he does is wait, then, he will have everything he needs to tend to his wounds."

"OK. Well, what happens?" I ask.

"The injured man doesn't like this. He thinks the young man is going to run off and not return, so he asks the young man if he can come with him to the store. The problem is, the young man is on his lunch break, and he needs to be fast to get back to work. If the injured man goes with him, he'll have to walk and be late, upsetting his employer. The injured man can't go with him because he can't keep up. Eventually, the young man convinces him to stay at the spot where they are talking. The young man runs as fast as he can a half a mile to the store. He pays twenty dollars for the bandages, the gauze, and the antibiotic ointment. He then runs another half mile back to the injured man, but when he arrives, the street corner where he told the injured man to wait for his return is empty. No one is there. The injured man did not wait for what he needed."

"Why did he leave?" the Rabbi asks.

Denim Guy throws up his hands. "Maybe he had to relieve himself. Maybe he got bored. Maybe someone else came along and gave him money. The point is the injured man allowed himself to get distracted. He did not wait until the appointed time of the young man's return. He left too early! And thus, he missed, by a mere matter of seconds, the very thing he most needed. Well, the young man, he can't believe it! He went out of his way to help this stranger, and now the stranger has disappeared. Time is running out. He's got to find the injured man to give him the bandages and medicine before he must be back at work. So, what does he do? The young man runs up and down the street looking for the stranger. He looks in all the shops and all the restaurants. He looks in the public restrooms and the bus stop. He asks other people if they've seen a man with an injured foot. But it's all for naught. The injured man is gone. He is not in any of the shops or cafes, he isn't in the restrooms or bus stops. He isn't at the park, or the post office. Dejected, the young man returns to work with a bag of medical supplies he does not need."

Rabbi Elihu nods his head. "The moral of the story: don't be in a rush! Don't think you have something when you haven't even received it yet. When it comes to studying text, if you think you have it figured it then you need to study longer. Chew on it! Savor the words. Make sure you see the seventy facets of the diamond. You gotta linger in the place where the treasure is found, make sure you looked in all the places, or else you might miss the one thing that changes your life forever."

Denim Guy and the Rabbi clink wine glasses. "Mozel Tov!" they say to each other.

The rest of the evening we eat and drink until I can't eat or drink any more. Then there is an exchange of gifts, which Denim Guy was kind enough to let me know of before I got on the plane. I've come prepared with a gift. Then there is singing and some dancing. And yes, even more debate, er, I mean ... dialogue.

EIGHTEEN
THE GOD FORUM

Marina Bay Sands, Singapore March 27th, 2036

"Ask me, Ethan."

"OK, will you heal my son?" "No."

I smile. This is how all our conversations begin now. He wants me to keep asking. I humor him, and don't mind the rejection. I've long since given up hope of a miracle for my Sam. I'm not one of Denim Guy's followers, but I keep asking because ... well, I don't know why.

We sit in the lobby of the Sands Expo building in Singapore, surrounded by the Sisters of Christ who dutifully watch over us. The entrance here is lined with palm trees. Representatives of all the world's major Jewish and Christian faith traditions have gathered to determine once and for all if The Forever Man is the Christ Messiah. The Pope is here, the College of Cardinals, Copts, Greek Orthodox, evangelical leaders, Reformed presbyters, authors, theologians, rabbis, basically the who's who of Judeo-Christian spirituality. They're calling it the God Forum, and they have all gathered to see and hear from one man, The Forever Man.

How did we get here? A month ago, I published my first piece on The Forever Man. We had reached the mid-point of our year together, so I figured it was time to show the world what I had learned and experienced in this man's presence. Within minutes of publication, it was the most-read article on the internet. Many were elated to read of what The Forever Man has said in private, and how he came to the world a second time. Others, many others, were troubled by what he said and did. This fomented arguments online about who was a true follower of Jesus. Disorder and confusion spread. A gathering of faith leaders was needed to sort it out. So here we are.

Several of the Forum's speakers nod to us as they walk to the convention hall.

"They think they have come here to judge me," Denim Guy says. "But I am here to judge them. All are here except the ones who gave themselves over to the allure of political power. These my father has given over to their idolatry, and I mourn their passing."

I glance at my phone. "We better get going. It's time."

Gathering my things, I fall in behind Denim Guy, who wants me to join him on stage. The Sisters of Christ escort us into the large bowl-shaped hall where thousands have gathered. A hush settles on the room as we enter. Led by women, Denim Guy walks across palm leaf-decorated carpet to the center of the bowl where a huge round table has been prepared. I squint as camera phones flash pictures in every direction.

The historic moment makes me recall something Denim Guy said months ago. It was back on our road trip on I-55 when he said he was wary of religious conclaves. Given how he is now entering a religious conclave, I wonder if it is a trap.

Denim Guy takes his seat at the table. I sit directly behind him, along with the Sisters of Christ, at a secondary ring of tables. TV cameras are set up around the crowd, recording live to the world every second of the God Forum. The Pope stands up to speak first.

"We are gathered here today, to find clarity on the issue of The Forever Man, with the desired outcome of some kind of consensus and unity. I have made my position clear. I believe this man to be the Christ, our Lord, The King of Kings, the Son of God, and the Son of Man."

When the Pope finishes speaking, the next person is up for an opening statement. This goes on for about an hour. Not every person at the oversized table speaks, but from a random draw, speakers are chosen from each of the faith traditions, and each offers their position on whether Denim Guy is really Jesus. By the time they are finished the Forum is evenly split on the question 50/50.

Finally, it's time for Denim Guy to speak.

He looks around at those gathered. "I see we are missing someone. Where is the representative of the poor? Do they not deserve a seat at the table?"

The crowd erupts into murmurs. The faith leaders turn to each other in confusion. Some of them look on the verge of panic, but Denim Guy waits for them to sort it out. He's left waiting for a while as they can't seem to find consensus on a way proceed.

The Pope seizes the moment and takes the initiative. "Yes, a representative of the poor is missing. Would The Forever Man have a recommendation?"

"If it pleases the Forum," Denim Guy responds, "I would seat Emily Tan Mei Ling. She is an usher here at this gathering."

This idea causes a commotion. Many of the leaders are not pleased. Some of them can barely hide their contempt. Others quietly look on, amused and intrigued. After some discussion, it is agreed to allow the usher a seat at the table of faith leaders. Her name is called out. Eventually, the timid, uniformed usher comes forward. Emily is a young Chinese woman with Down's syndrome. Denim Guy stands up as she approaches. The other faith leaders follow suit. Seeing The Forever Man, Emily runs up to him and greets him with a big hug. Another chair is added to the table, and Emily takes her seat like an honored guest.

In stunned silence, the rest of the Forum take their seats. "Now," says Denim Guy. "We may begin."

One of the theologians stands up. "No one can deny the miracles you have done. But the people I represent wonder about your theology. We know full well that our theology is not perfect, still, we must follow

1 John 4:1 and test you to see if you are from God, or, if you are a false prophet, another false Christ. Is this acceptable?"

Denim Guy flips on his microphone. "It is."

"You have done wonderful things, but it is still unclear where you stand on the issue of sin and salvation."

"No one can come to the father except through me," Denim Guy begins. "I am the Way, the Truth, and the Life. I require people to repent of the sins which they are conscious of, and not sins of which they are ignorant, or extra rules concocted by men."

"And what about homosexuality? Abortion? Sex before marriage? Pornography?"

"Ask the one who has been with me from the beginning." Denim Guy turns to me. "Have I condoned any of these things?"

I clear my throat and step up to the microphone. "Technically, no, he has not. But-"

"So, what is it that bothers you?" Denim Guy leans back in his chair. "I will tell you. It is not my ethics, or my theology. It is my love. I love sinners, and you find it troublesome."

Grumbling can be heard on the other side of the table. They did not like this response. Another man stands up. He looks to be from the conservative evangelical group judging by the look of him.

"Our issue …" He pauses. "Well, one of our issues is eschatology. Your Second Coming has not been at all like what we expected. You also speak like you are a *woke* Christian. You elevate women to spiritual leadership, denigrate patriarchy, champion social justice and CRT, ridicule our ministries. I could go on …"

"Is it not loving to correct someone?" Denim Guy asks. "This is what you say when you chastise unbelievers. Can the chastiser not also be chastised as an act of love? There is this saying in the 21st century: you can dish it out, but you can't take it."

A few people in the audience laugh. The evangelical questioner sits down.

"As for the way I came here," Denim Guy continues. "I did come on the clouds with power and glory, so why didn't you notice? You know the answer. You were too busy and weren't looking for me."

Other leaders around the table stand up and have their say. They each take their turn airing their theological issues with The Forever Man.

Denim Guy finally holds up his hand, signaling he has heard enough. "The problem with all of you is that you separate theology and action. This is impossible. They are one and the same. My actions are my theology. I serve the poor. I love sinners. I speak the truth. I patiently bear with foolishness. I give justice to the oppressed. I restore the broken. I tear down strongholds of oppression. I AM love. You are right in saying your theology is not perfect, it is very flawed. Even now, in your hearts you prefer your own theology, rather than the God who sits before you, your Maker. I see you searching for excuses. Your allegiance is to your opinions. How is it you know the scriptures, but you don't know me? Still, there is hope. There is one among you who does have perfect theology. There is one here who has not erred in what they believe or do. Would that person please stand up."

The leaders sit up in their chair. They flip through their Bibles and pull out their position papers. The rabbis discuss with themselves. The cardinals and the Pope confer. The Pentecostals hold up their hands and murmur in tongues.

A Reformed theologian stands up and opens his mouth to speak.

"Not you," Denim Guy interjects. The Reformed theologian sits back down.

The Pentecostals come forward. "Nope."

They sit back down, dejected.

Other groups try to make their case, but none of them are the one. Pretty soon, anyone else who hasn't come forward is too scared to get openly rejected.

Exasperated, Denim Guy takes a deep breath. "Emily," he announces. The crowd gasps. "Please stand." She looks at The Forever Man in uncertainty. He smiles in encouragement, and motions for her to get up.

"Emily, would you tell the group your theology. Tell us what you think is true about God. It's OK."

The young woman thinks for a moment, then her face lights up, as if the happiest thought popped into her head.

Her sweet face beaming with joy, Emily begins to sing. *"Jesus loves me, this I know, for the Bible tells me so. Little ones to Him belong, they are weak, but he is strong! Yes, Jesus loves me, yes, Jesus loves me, yes, Jesus loves me. My Jesus loves me so."*

Stunned, the crowd applauds, but it was the kind of applause that sounds unsure, like the crowd knows it should clap, but doesn't know why. Emily gives Denim Guy another hug. This time she doesn't let go. He gladly cradles her in his arms.

"You see?" Denim Guy asks the gathering. "No degrees, no agenda, no position papers. Just perfect theology. The Kingdom belongs to her. If only you could be more like Emily, it can belong to you too."

Emily's song has quite an effect on the leaders at the table. One had the sense that they came to this meeting armed for battle, but the voice of the poor had disarmed them. Now they are listening more than speaking. They have shelved their papers. The Catholics are talking with the Protestants, the Pentecostals with the left-leaning mainline churches, the rabbis with the Orthodox Christians, and everyone in between.

The rest of the meeting there is a lighter mood. Denim Guy sits and answers every question, all while cradling Emily in his arms. By the end of the Forum the overwhelming majority of the leaders vote to affirm The Forever Man as the Christ, the Son of God, Head of the Church, King of Kings, and Lord of Lords.

Hours later—and still holding Emily—Denim Guy leaves the meeting to adoration. The crowd is crying out to Jesus. They press in to touch just a thread of his denim clothing, or the soles of his shoes as they traverse the carpet palm leaves. Even I can feel a sense of relief. At last, there was consensus among Denim Guy's believers. For the first time in 2,000 years, the Church was united.

NINETEEN
TEARS IN VALHALLA

British Columbia, Canada April 8th, 2036

"Don't say it," I say into my phone. The face of Denim Guy fills the screen. He looks about to spit out the words, but then smiles and says nothing. A picturesque background of mountains and blue sky is behind him.

I sit at my son's bedside, adjusting his teddy bear so it lays right under his arm, just the way he wants. Over the phone, I give Denim Guy a rundown on my son's health status. Sam is in good spirits; we are here at Barnes Jewish for a round of tests. I know the next thing Denim Guy is going to say, so I preempt him.

"Zip it." I make the zip motion with my fingers moving across my lips. "Don't do it. Don't ask me to ask you again. Please. By the way, where are you? The Alps?"

"Good guess, but no." Denim Guy turns the camera toward the mountain. "This is Valhalla Provincial Park in Canada. I'm here taking a little retreat before things get crazy."

"Looks beautiful," I comment. "Hope I can see it in person someday."

"Why not right now?" Denim Guy asks.

The call ends. I look at the time 2:47 pm. I feel a familiar sensation. "No wait, wait—"

My body ... *jolts*, or shifts, and next thing I know I'm standing next to Denim Guy in the mountain paradise of Valhalla Provincial Park.

"Why did you do that?" I demand. "I need to be with my son. Any minute now the nurse is coming."

"No worries, my friend." Denim Guy pats my shoulder. "I took the liberty of taking you off the train for a little bit."

"The train?"

"You recall our discussion of time, yes?"

"Um, yeah." I look around at the mountains, the crystal-clear lake, the blue sky. "So ... what, am I outside of time? How does this work?"

"Kind of." Denim Guy sits down next to a campfire a few paces away. "Come here and sit. Let's talk. When we are done, I'll get you back on board the train and return you to the hospital at the same time you left."

I throw up my hands in exasperation. I take a seat at the campfire, warming up my hands even though, now that I think about it, I'm not really cold.

"Why are you still here, Ethan?" "You mean—"

"Why do you still talk to me? By all accounts, many would think what I have done to you is cruel. To keep on asking you to ask me to heal your son without saying yes would be like torture, like I'm playing with you, prolonging your pain. So, why are you here?"

Sparks go up from the logs as I think. "It would *seem* that way," I reply. "But I don't believe in God, never served God, so it seems unfair that I should come seeking a hand-out I haven't deserved. Besides, the treatments are working. Sam is getting better. Well, that is to say, his quality of life has improved. His appetite has returned somewhat. He can play video games. Since we've met, he hasn't suffered much. Science is amazing. The medicines we have are remarkable. We've come a long way from leeches and drinking kerosene."

"Indeed." Denim Guy studies me. "Who do you say I am then, Ethan Tellinger?"

I shrug. "A freak of nature. I honestly don't know. I do know one thing. You are a man. I can see you, feel you, smell your breath. I can't explain how I got here, or how you can move mountains and make manna fall from the sky. Your influence over people is unique, but not necessarily miraculous. Are you God in the flesh? I don't know if I can go there, even after everything I've seen. In the end, maybe I'm just not a man of faith."

"Everyone must have faith in something," he replies. "Even if it is the faith that God does not exist."

The idea of healing recalls a question I have been wanting to ask. "It does make me wonder though. You can do all these miraculous things, so why don't you heal people more often? Why not empty out all the hospitals, or cure cancer?"

"I did not come to heal; I came to resurrect. Mankind needs saving from themselves, not saving from cancer. Even so, cancer, disease, illness, frailty, old age … all these things are passing away. They will be no more in the new world I am creating. The old ways of the curse shall cease to be."

"When?"

"When the Second Born of the Dead comes forth."

None of this makes any sense to me. "Well, at least now there is consensus in the Church. The God Forum settled it, right?"

"We shall see." Denim Guy stares into the fire and folds his hands. "Peter swore allegiance to me, then denied me three times when I was arrested. The Church will face the same test. They will have their chance to stand by me when next I am arrested."

"Wait, what? You're going to be arrested? When? How?"

"My Kingdom is not of this world, Ethan Tellinger. It is only a matter of time before they collide. Will those who affirmed me at the God Forum stand by me when this happens? They will be forced to choose. Will they hold on to what they believe, or will they wilt under pressure?"

"This new world you keep talking about, what is it? Like some kind of *utopia*?"

"No. Utopia is a man-made fantasy of man-made perfection. My new world is not a fantasy, and it will not reflect human ideas of perfection."

Neither of us says anything for a while, and I'm content with that. All this talk of riddles and new worlds is interesting, but for now, it's all talk. There's nothing that can be done about it. If Denim Guy wants to play his cards close to his chest, then that's his prerogative. We stare into the campfire.

"By the way," says Denim Guy, breaking the silence. "Your wife says 'hello.'" He looks over at me and my jaw hanging wide open. "She was a follower of mine. You knew this."

"Well, yeah but—"

"She has been praying for you."

Thrown off by the sudden mention of my wife, I take a beat to put my thoughts and emotions together. "Vivian died giving birth to Sam. She was the love of my life." I can't shake the feeling that I'm being manipulated. "What's your play here? Use my dead wife to get me to believe in you?"

"On the contrary, it was Vivian who convinced me." "Convinced of you what?"

"That you are a man of faith. No one else knows you like she does."

"Knows me? Did know me, you mean. She died. Her faith didn't save her. Or … what? Her soul lived on? Well, where is she then? Let me guess, strumming a harp up in heaven?"

"Where is heaven?" Denim Guy asks. "Seriously. It's a real place, so where is it? Can you go up into Earth's atmosphere and find it? No. Heaven is a spiritual reality. It exists beyond and alongside the physical realm. You ask where she is. She is here, everywhere. I came from the place she is in now."

"Fine," I say, barely containing my contempt. "I think once you're dead, you're dead. But go on. Anything else Vivian wants to say to me?"

"Yes. She mentioned a garden. The Garden of the Sun Singer."

The name of that place spoken out loud causes a pit in my stomach. "What did you say?"

"The Garden of the Sun Singer, at Allerton Park, in Monticello, IL."

"I know where it is! How do you know about the Sun Singer?" "It's where Vivian first told you she was pregnant with Sam. You were having a picnic by the statue of the Sun Singer. She hid the ultrasound photos inside the picnic basket. She says it was the happiest moment of her life, and she would do it all over again with you."

Drops of cold wetness fall from my cheeks and onto my hands. "The Garden of the Sun Singer was a special place for us. We would go there in the fall and picnic. I still remember the crunch of purple leaves underneath our feet. In the afternoon I would take a nap. Vivian would write in her journal. The Sun Singer was our escape, it's where we met, where we talked, where I proposed, where we got married—"

"Where you asked me to heal her," Denim Guy says softly. "When the doctors said there was something wrong."

"And where you didn't answer." I can't help but laugh. "You know, I really believed too. I believed because Vivian believed. What young fools we were. You know, that's one of the hardest things. It's not just the loss, it's the feeling like an idiot because you put your hope in imaginary things."

Denim Guy says nothing. He looks at the flames, the yellow light reflecting off his brown eyes.

"The Sun Singer is where I lost whatever faith I had. When Vivian died, I promised never to ask God for another thing. Never again would I be made a fool. I thought it would be easy to ask for your help when we first met. You were just another mystic. I was curious, but the more we talked, the more I felt like I was back in the Garden of the Sun Singer. I couldn't place it at the time, but something didn't seem right. I couldn't ask you."

I glance at my fireside companion for a reaction. He looks back at me, studying my face.

"Well, don't you have something wise or spiritual to say?" "Ethan …"

"Don't. Don't say it." I stand up to leave. "Ask me."

"Enough! Take me back to the hospital."

"The Sun Singer," says Denim Guy standing up with me. "By Carl Milles 1875-1955, a 15'2" bronze statue of Apollo, his arms outstretched to greet the morning sky with song. The sculpture is one of three. The second is in Stockholm, the third is in National Memorial Park near Washington, DC. The Allerton Park Sun Singer was Milles' favorite. It stands on a pedestal adapted from the symbolic Altar of Heaven in Peking."

"Why are you telling me this?"

"I was there. You were not a fool to ask me then. You are not a fool to ask me now. Do you know what you are? You are an altar. The place where gifts and sacrifices are offered up to me. The place where I lay down and die. You, Ethan. My Altar of Heaven."

"No, all you have is more riddles."

"Who would I be if all I did was what you wanted when you wanted it?" Denim Guy pleads. "What would I become if everything I said always made sense to you? I'd be your creation. The truth is that no answer I give will satisfy you, and no answer *should* satisfy you. That's OK. My grace is sufficient for your anger at me. Anyone can serve me in the light. Few there are who can serve me in the dark. Many want to sacrifice for me, be great for me, be lifted up for me. Not many are content to be an altar for me so that I can be lifted up and draw all people to myself. Just as I stooped down to become a wiggling baby in a barn, so I ask you to do the same. I ask you to follow me. I search the earth for those who want to be, like that Catholic priest once said, 'a manger not a manager,' an altar not an all-star."

I find this so tedious and exasperating. "It's all just words. We humans are your little playthings, aren't we? There always has to be some deeper meaning, some new hoop to jump through. Meanwhile my wife is dead!"

"In me, death is more life, not less. At this very moment, Vivian is more alive than you are, Ethan Tellinger."

"Then where is she!?" I push Denim Guy and he staggers backward. "I want to see her. I want to touch her. This is being alive: touching, seeing, feeling, smelling, hearing. This is life."

"I am life!" Denim Guy beats his fist against his chest. "I SEE Vivian. I HEAR Vivian. I can hold her, smell her, *feel* her living. Why? Because whoever trusts in me will live, even though they die. I AM the life, and I give life. I give life to the bacteria in your stomach and the microbes on your skin. I breathed life into the first human. From the depths of the ocean to the farthest galaxy I give life to all. You are not a pawn. I am not playing with you. One day your grief will end. I will wipe away every tear."

I clap my hands in his face. "Well, good for you. What do you want then, hm? What's the catch?"

"No catch. I want you to abide in me, Ethan. Abide in me in the good memories and the bad memories. Abide in me when I answer and when I don't answer. Abide in me at the weddings and in the hospitals. Abide in me and you will be where I created you to be, doing what I created you to do. This is true humility. It is not thinking of yourself less or thinking less of yourself, it is abiding in me, remaining with me. You want to move on, to be active, to be done, to move out from under, to progress to another season of life. But I have not called you to move or to progress, I have called you to abide, to stay. But the truth is you can't abide because abiding feels like giving up. It feels like surrender. It feels that way because it IS that way. This, Ethan, is living by faith."

"How about you?" I counter. "Where do you have to remain? Tell me, where does the King of Kings and Lord of Lords have to abide?"

"Here." Denim Guy points to my chest. "And here." He points to my head. "I want to abide in you. I want to abide in the sad you, the depressed you, the anxious you, the sinner that is you, the confused, discontent, angry you. I want to abide in the you that doesn't want to abide at all. Abiding, remaining still, produces fruit. It is not work that produces, it is abiding. I told you before, I am the Vine, my followers are the branches. A branch does not labor, or manage, or decide, or venture off to do great things. A branch does not get credit. A branch is not noticed. A branch is not glorified. A branch remains hidden. A branch abides. It is the fruit that is seen, not the branch. A branch does nothing but remain attached in the vine. For a branch, most days are the same. The scenery is the same. There is not much going on. Every day is dull and repetitive. Some days it rains. Some days it storms. Some days are sunny and warm, and flowers bloom. Some days are dark and cold, and the leaves fall. But a branch remains attached to the vine through it all. If the branch is cut off, it withers and dies. So, this is life, being a branch in all seasons. Ethan, the events of your life were designed to lead you to me, to this very moment."

"I still don't understand the purpose of my wife's death, or death in general. Why does anyone have to die?"

"Maybe death IS the purpose of life?"

"Oh, that's not morbid at all." I say it with as much sarcasm as possible.

"The moment you're born you are doomed to face death. When a person takes up their cross to follow me, they die every day, and are thus fitted for death."

"I thought the purpose of life was to know you and tell other people about you. That's what they say in church, or at least, when I went to church that's what they said. *'To know Him and make Him known'* goes the saying. They repeat that everywhere. It's kind of annoying."

"The purpose of life cannot be reduced to a catchphrase. All sorts of nonsense has been happening in the church for the sake of *mission*. Well, sorry to disappoint, but the purpose of life is mystery. Not knowing the purpose IS the purpose. God's plan is best understood when it is not known, but rather, experienced. Freedom is not in knowing something, freedom is in the grace to abide. Just abide. Abide here. Abide there. Abide now. Abide later. Abide in pain. Abide in joy. Abide in boredom. Abide with what happened. Abide without knowing what comes next. Abide in me, if you can. But know this, no one can abide in me without abiding in affliction and the uncertainty of death. And many who DO abide in me have not the ability to make me known to other people. Are they less for not being able? Certainly not. Indeed, they are my most precious creations. Your abilities do not give you value. People have value simply because they are people. I want them to abide in me, and I in them. Never more do they abide in me than when they do not know life's purpose."

I throw up my hands. "So, tell me, how does one go about *abiding* in you?"

Denim Guy gives me a wry look.

"Oh, come on." I turn my back and roll my eyes. "You told me not to say it."

"I'm done asking, understand? I told you I'd follow you around for a year. Well, the year is almost over. I will continue to cover you for work because my editor is expecting me to write part two of the feature. But after that I'm done, get it?"

"As you wish."

I clear my throat "Good. Now, put me back on the tr—"

The mountains *shift*. I feel that familiar jolt sensation. In the blink of an eye, I'm back in the hospital room with Sam in St. Louis. I look at the time on my phone. It's 2:47 pm, the same time I left. I breathe a sigh of relief and run my hands through my hair.

"Everything all right, Dad?"

"Hey buddy." I grab his hand. "Yeah, I'm fine. Don't you worry about me. How are you?"

"I'm OK," Sam says, his eyes getting droopy. "Where did you go?"
"Uh, what do you mean?" I ask. "I've been right here."

"I thought you … went somewhere." His eyes close. The meds are kicking in. "Dad?"

"I'm here, buddy." My phone falls on the floor as I move to lay down with Sam on the bed. He stirs a little bit.

"I could hear Mom," Sam mumbles. "She was singing to me."
"OK Sammy. OK."

The nurse comes in.

She gives me a thumbs up. "I think we're ready," she whispers. I kiss my son on the forehead. "Here we go Sammy."

TWENTY
VIACRUCIS DEL MIGRANTE

San Pedro Sula, Honduras April 29th, 2036

FLIES. HEAT. EXHAUSTION. REPEAT.

Weeks after our visit in Valhalla, I have agreed to go on my last trip with Denim Guy. He's zapped me to Honduras, where he is traveling with a migrant caravan. The Via Crucis Del Migrante they call it. The Stations of the Cross of the Migrant, roughly translated. They consist of mostly women and children. It's about fleeing the dangers of Honduras, more than pursuing the American dream. For these people, it seemed that movement was the dream, a kind of "anywhere but here" mentality because *here* is where their children are kidnapped, where they are raped, and murdered, and starved, and exploited.

There is no transportation. The days are spent walking in the heat, and the insects, minute by minute, hour by hour, on repeat day after day inching closer to the US—Mexico border. We rest in an abandoned soccer field outside San Pedro Sula. Denim Guy goes to each man, woman, and child in the caravan and gives them water from a canteen that never goes dry. For food the caravan eats the manna, which follows them wherever they go.

As for myself and Denim Guy, we haven't spoken much since our last meeting. I take photos, interview members of the caravan, help out where needed. They are all tired and afraid. The caravan is constantly in danger of gangs and criminals harassing them as they trudge through the jungle from town to town. It sends a shiver down my spine when I think about if my son were stuck in a place like this.

"We must get moving," says Denim Guy, helping exhausted migrants to their feet nearby. "Vamos, Señora. Vamos."

Zombies is what they all look like, so tired they move in a daze. But the moment Denim Guy touches them it's as if they are shocked by jumper cables. The fog is lifted. What little possessions they have are gathered up, and they start walking again.

I help a mother with her three young children. Slinging my bag behind my back I push a stroller carrying a sleeping toddler.

Denim Guy comes up behind me. "Thank you for coming, Ethan. These people are near to my heart, the heart of God."

We shake hands. "What exactly is the plan here?" I ask. "Just keep on walking?"

"For a little while longer," Denim Guy replies. "We are almost to our destination.'

"Which is?"

"A crossroad." He points northward, to a place up the road. "A few miles away. There is a young man in trouble that we must help, then we can go to the fording place."

Yards turn into miles. Hours pass. No one talks. Even the children stay silent. Everyone is too tired to even speak. There is no sound save for the flies and the occasional sound of a palm smacking an insect.

The monotony of the walk is broken by a commotion up front. All of a sudden migrants begin running in the opposite direction. Denim Guy and I run up to the head of the caravan. Immediately we see the source of the panic. About three hundred yards ahead the road is blocked by vehicles and men holding machine guns. Frightened migrants disperse into the jungle. Denim Guy calms everyone down, giving instructions in Spanish. The terror in the eyes of the women and children is heart-breaking, but those that remain hold together and wait on the road. A few migrants come back out of the jungle. For now, the caravan holds.

"Come with me," Denim Guy says. He starts walking toward the armed men.

I assume he's talking to me.

Ten paces and I catch up to him. "Let me guess, one of these gangbangers is the young man we need to help."

"Correct."

Guns click loaded as we approach. Eight Honduran men stand in front of small trucks outfitted with .50 caliber machine guns in the truck beds. The men wear bandanas, cargo shorts, and dirty graphic tees with the sleeves cut off. They point their guns at us and shout something in Spanish.

Not even flinching or showing any sign of hesitation, Denim Guy keeps walking forward.

"Deténganse o dispararemos!" yells a bearded man in sunglasses, his AK-47 waving around.

Denim Guy doesn't respond, just keeps walking. He doesn't seem threatened, so I keep following.

The bearded man pulls the trigger on his AK. The weapon jams. "Abran fuego!" he shouts to his companions. "Llevátelos! Llevátelos!"

Gang members look at each other in confusion as they try to fire their weapons to no avail. All of their guns have suddenly jammed. They throw down the guns and unsheathe machetes. Mouths are peeled back in rage revealing filed teeth as they charge at us, blades drawn.

A few steps are as far as they get when they become frozen mid-attack. Denim Guy never breaks his stride as he nonchalantly moves around the suspended-in-time gang members. Somehow, I have the wherewithal to snap a photo of one of the unmoving and incapacitated Hondurans, their legs stuck in the air mid-stride. I've come to expect this kind of thing from The Forever Man, but it is still unnerving.

"Come out of the truck, Miguel." Denim Guy patiently waits beside the bearded man, whose mouth is stuck open in the middle of shouting orders, his eyes flickering around in paralyzed panic.

I see a head pop up in the window of one of the trucks. The door opens. A boy falls out of the cab. He looks around at the snow-globed gang members in stunned silence.

The boy snaps his fingers in a gang member's face. "Qué diablura es esta?"

"It is not the devil, Miguel." Denim Guy steps around a gang member to reveal himself. "It's me. The Forever Man. You know me, yes?"

Miguel nervously rubs his hands on his flannel shirt. He wiggles his head in the affirmative, his greasy hair dangling in front of his youthful face.

Denim Guy gets down on one knee. "Do not be afraid. These men cannot hurt you anymore. We are going to the US border. Do you want to come with us?"

Raindrops plop on the vehicles and jungle leaves. Weeping, Miguel covers his face. He falls into the arms of Denim Guy.

"Ellos me lastimaron mucho," he says through the tears.

Denim Guy strokes his head. "I know, but I am greater than the hurt they caused you." He looks up to the sky. "Father, our beloved one is hurt. Let the favor you have given to me now pass to him. What trauma he has endured, let it be given to me. Amen."

Miguel lets out a deep breath, as if a great weight has been lifted off him. He wipes his face and stands up.

"Gracias, señor Jesus," he says with folded hands. "Gracias."

We give Miguel some water and manna that I had packed in my bag. He shoves the white bread into his mouth as we walk back to the caravan.

Instructions are given to the migrants to gather around Denim Guy who is holding Miguel's hand. My Spanish is not very good, but at length the members of the caravan begin to lay hands on Denim Guy. Those who can't reach him lay hands on the person in front of them. The person behind them lays a hand on their shoulder until everyone, man, woman, and child are physically linked together.

"You too, Ethan." Denim Guy gives me a nod. I place a hand on his shoulder.

"Everyone ready? Todos listos?"

"Sí," some of the migrants say with a look of expectation in their tired eyes.

"Listo," say some of the men, and "lista," say some of the women.

Denim Guy smiles. "OK, here we go."

The jungle *shivers.* The clouds boil. The road writhes. The shifting-like sensation pushes me, pushes all of us. In the blink of an eye, the jungle and road are gone. Sand blows through the joined-together caravan. Immediately we shield our eyes from the sun. When our eyes adjust to the sudden light, we look around to see we have been transported to a desert. Blackbrush acacia shrubs surround the group, along with agave plants, yucca trees, and some flowering senna.

"We're here," says Denim Guy.

I fan some sand away from my face. "Where is here?"

"The Chihuahuan Desert." Denim Guy disappears into the brush for a moment.

The migrants do not appear to be fazed at all by our miraculous teleportation. It occurs to me now that they might have experienced this before with The Forever Man.

"This way." Denim Guy's hand appears above a bush and motions us forward. "Over here. Follow me."

We collect our things and follow his voice, carefully watching out for thorns and snakes. I bring up the tail end of the caravan. A few yards through the brush I begin to hear rushing water. Further in, the vegetation thins out and I see the migrants all lined up staring at a river.

My shirt acts as a rag to wipe my brow. "Is that …?"

"Yes," says Denim Guy coming up behind me. "The Rio Grande River. The land on the other side is the United States, our destination. These people will be able to seek asylum there."

One problem with this that I notice. "How do we get across? I don't see any boats."

"Easy." Denim Guy steps around me to the edge of the river. "We walk." He steps out onto the water without sinking. Denim Guy is walking on water.

"Come on," he says, beckoning us to follow. "It's alright. I won't let you sink."

Miguel ventures out first. He taps the water with his shoe. His leg bends as he applies his weight to the water. A toothy smile comes across his face when he doesn't sink. Miguel runs to Denim Guy. They embrace in the middle of the Rio Grande. A mother pushes her stroller onto the water. It rolls smoothly along the surface of the brown water without sinking. One by one the migrants walk out onto the water. I walk out with them on the water, but first testing the surface. I lift my foot to feel the bottom of my boot. It wasn't even wet. Completely dry. Why should I even be surprised. I'm not, but I am at the same time. How is this possible?

Together, the whole caravan follows Denim Guy. We walk upon the waters the entire 300-yard width of the river, the children running around the surface of the water, laughing and playing.

On the US side we disembark the river with dry shoes. The kids want to stay on the water and play. It takes some coaxing, but eventually we are all on the other side. We climb the bank and come out near a dirt road. There is a palpable sense of relief in the caravan. They've made it. For the first time in their lives, freedom and safety are possible.

"Where do we go now?" I ask.

"Nowhere." Denim Guy plops himself down on the ground. "We wait for border patrol to arrive."

The muffled sound of an engine is heard in the distance. Light brown dust puffs up on the horizon.

I shield my eyes from the sun. "We don't have to wait long. Look." The group looks to where I'm pointing to the northwest. Marked vehicles slide to a halt on the road. Border Patrol agents exit the cars, guns drawn.

"Get on the ground!" they shout at us.

"Do as they say," Denim Guy tells us. He stands up and walks to the agents, his hands held up. "It's all right," he says to the agents. "They are seeking asylum. I escorted them across."

The agents either don't hear him or don't care. Denim Guy is forced to his knees and handcuffed. They lay him down face down in the dust.

Shouting in Spanish, the agents round up the rest of the caravan. Mothers are being arrested. The children are crying and terrified of the border patrol agents. Feeling helpless I look to Denim Guy.

"Come on, help us!" I yell at him. He just lays there in the sand, unmoving. How is this happening? An agent shoves me in the back, and I fall to the ground. "I know those cuffs can't hold you. Get up! Do something!"

"I'm sorry, Ethan." Denim Guy is hauled to his feet. "This is the way it must happen. I have broken the law."

TWENTY-ONE
LETTERS FROM DETENTION

Presidio Station, Texas April 31st, 2036

MY PHONE DINGS. IT'S the hourly vitals report for Sam. The hospital has developed an app linking his heart rate, body temp, respiratory rate, and blood pressure straight to my phone so I know how he is doing at all times. The past ten months it has been a lifesaver while I have been away, only slightly reducing the guilt I feel every time I leave to cover The Forever Man. The doctors and nurses reassure me that parents have faced similar dilemmas of balancing work and being there for their children. I'm a single parent with no immediate family. My sick days have all been used. If I take a leave of absence, we lose our insurance. This past year the app has been my only connection to my son when I have to travel.

Thanks to my US citizenship, press credentials, and a good lawyer, I've been released by the border patrol. Denim Guy and the rest of the caravan remain locked in cages at the Presidio Station where we were transported. Currently their fate is unknown. They are claiming asylum, so their case will have to be heard by a judge, but who knows when that will be. As for Denim Guy …

"Mr. Tellinger?" asks a border agent. "Yes?"

"This way."

I sling my bag over my shoulder. The agent leads me through the station to an area where the apprehended migrants are being held. This part of the facility resembles a large garage partitioned by chain-linked fence. The floor is concrete. There is little ventilation. The caravan we arrived with is at the far end of the building. I see they've been given blankets, food, water bottles, formula, diapers, and some other toiletries. Denim Guy is in a six-by-six holding cage adjacent to the migrants. He is crouched on the floor but stands up when I approach.

"Thirty minutes, OK?" says the agent.

"Got it."

"I'll be over here if you need anything." The agent leaves to stand guard in the corridor between cages.

"I'm glad to see you have been released," says Denim Guy in hushed tones. He reaches into his shirt and pulls out some envelopes. "I want you to take these and mail them."

The border agent is looking away, so I snatch the envelopes. "What are they?" I ask.

"Letters I have written. The addresses are already there. You will recognize the names. You've met them before: June from Skid Row, Lisa, the Sisters of Christ, Pastor Abraham, Macarius the Prisoner—"

"Big Mac?"

"… the Widow of Jenin, and Emily, the usher at the God Forum in Singapore. I have chosen them to be the seven golden lampstands that will lead my church in the age to come when I redeem the world."

"Lampstands?" I stuff the letters in my bag. "Never mind, I'll make sure they get mailed. Can I ask you something? Why are you still here? I've seen your powers. You can leave whenever you want."

"It is necessary that I stay. They are going to charge me with crimes, and there must be a trial."

"Crimes? What crimes?"

Denim Guy raises an eyebrow and shrugs. "I'm not seeking asylum, so, take your pick: 8 USC 1325 Improper Entry by an Alien, 8 USC 1324 Smuggling and Harboring Aliens, Avoidance of Examination by Customs, the list goes on. But fear not, I have overcome the world. I will redeem all of creation."

Heart palpitations beat against my chest as it suddenly dawns on me that I may be guilty of these crimes too.

"Don't worry," says Denim Guy noticing my panic. "You were along for the ride. You didn't know where I was taking you. You are not guilty, my friend. But these are just the crimes I committed in the United States. The whole world will judge me now because of the people I have helped and the miracles I have wrought. It has not been decided yet, but events have been set in motion. I will be taken to The Hague for crimes of aggression."

"What? Why? How? That doesn't even make sense. All you've done is go about the world doing good. I was there. I witnessed it. I can vouch for you. And besides, the US has traditionally opposed the ICC because they don't use a jury trial system. This outcome you are describing is highly unlikely."

"It will not matter. The world hates me. It has always hated me. They will come together and find a way to accuse me and judge me and count me among the criminals. You will see for yourself when they broadcast the trial live on TV for the whole world to witness. For you, Ethan Tellinger, the time has come for you to be with Sam."

I don't like the sound of that. "I'm sorry, but what is that supposed to mean?"

Denim Guy leans against the cage and stares at his scarred hands. "You have been with me enough. Our year is almost over, but not yet. The Second Born of the Dead is coming next, then the Awakening. The new world is at hand, my Kingdom. But first I must be accused and found guilty by the world powers. All sorts of vile things they will say about me. You know the truth, Ethan. You have seen me in public and in private. All I have said has been on the record. Look what happened here. I helped these people with food and water, I protected them, gave them dignity and justice. All who come to me will never hunger or thirst. And yet I am a criminal for doing so. Ever has it been this way."

"Are you really going to let them throw you in prison? The churches at the God Forum will come to your defense. That's hundreds of millions of people. They will fight for you."

"No," Denim Guy replies. "They must not, and they will not. The governments of the earth must be allowed to do what their heart desires to do, but the government is on my shoulders. Their scheme is to judge me, but I will judge them for all the world to see. Do they welcome the stranger, feed the hungry, clothe the naked, care for the sick, visit the prisoner, do justice for the poor and marginalized? Do they lift up the oppressed and love their neighbor? Did they protect the weak and hold the strong and wealthy accountable? This is how I will judge."

"Hm. A lot of governments aren't going to fair very well then."

On this at least we agree. Neither of us say anything for a time. I decide to share something though that has been weighing on my mind. "I finally figured it out," I say at last. "Your name. The Forever Man."

"And?"

"My initial thought was it being about something more spiritual or theological. But then I started to think about all the times this past year I have had to wait on you while you talked with people. Then it hit me: the name was more down to earth. You are The Forever Man, because you take forever to listen to people and their stories, their complaints and fears and hopes and dreams. I think that's what strikes me most about you. It isn't the miracles or the wisdom or your all-powerful, all- knowing identity. For me, it's the love you have for people that has made an impression on me. You love people and make them feel loved. I realize now, I haven't ever really loved people, not the way you do. I don't really listen, or if I do listen, I listen in a way that is just waiting for the other person to stop talking so I can speak. I'm always looking to get out of conversations, or if I enjoy a conversation, I can't help but psychoanalyze what I said. I'm too aware of myself to listen, too aware of myself to love. That's what I envy about you. You don't seem aware of yourself when people are around. All your attention is on them."

"It's true." Denim Guy leans against the cage and folds his arms. "I do take forever visiting with people. It can drive others crazy how long I can listen! Generally, I am slow to speak, too slow for many people."

"No kidding." I crack a smile. "I'm living proof of that." We share a laugh.

"And you see what happens when I am here in the flesh. There's not enough of me to go around. But I am here also in my followers. If you know my true followers then you know me, and if you know me, then you know my father. All over the world people can experience The Forever Man, experience Jesus, through my disciples. So, yes, you are correct, and sorry to disappoint, but The Forever Man name, it is just a reference to my hospitality and my love. I like to hear what interests people. I feel what they feel when they speak. I impart this gift to my people, that they can listen and love and be hospitable like me. No one who hates is my disciple, no matter how many times they invoke the name of Jesus, or how vast their knowledge of the Bible. Some parts of the Bible are hard to understand. It's OK to admit that. What matters is love and kindness, gentleness and respect, honor and hospitality, justice, and peace. Upon these rest all the law and theology."

Our visit time is almost up. We exchange goodbyes, and I realize I don't know when I will see this extraordinary man again, or if I *will* see him again.

"Well," I look at the time on my phone. "If you are God, then God really is ... love."

Denim Guy looks shocked. "Ethan Tellinger, are you becoming a believer?"

"Hey, you never know with me ..."

The border patrol agent comes back. I turn away to leave.

"Ethan."

I turn back to him. "Yes?"

He peers at me through the cage, that familiar knowing look in his eyes. "Thank you."

"For what?"

"For being with me."

"Alright, let's go." The border patrol agent holds out his arm to escort me out.

Whether he meant to thank me for being with him now, or for the last year I'm left to wonder. At the far end of the facility, I take one last look at Denim Guy, The Forever Man. Through several panels of fencing, I can barely make out his Middle Eastern features still watching me as I go.

TWENTY-TWO
THE PROSECUTOR V. THE FOREVER MAN

International Criminal Court, The Hague, Netherlands June 28th, 2036

"ALL RISE," ANNOUNCES THE court usher on the hospital room television. Everyone stands up.

The news anchor touches his ear. "We now go live to The Hague for the long-awaited trial of The Forever Man, at one time one of the world's most popular and beloved figures. He now sits in handcuffs before Presiding Judge Mathieu, and two others judges on the panel. Let's listen."

"Please be seated," says the court usher, after all the judges have taken their seats.

I turn up the volume, but not too much. In the weeks since Presidio Station I have published part II of my time with Denim Guy and the article is the talk of the internet. Despite the success, I haven't been able to enjoy it. Sam's health has taken a turn for the worse. For reasons the doctors cannot explain, the effectiveness of the treatments is starting to wane. So, we find ourselves back at Barnes Jewish Hospital in St. Louis. Sam is resting peacefully now. Most of the day he sleeps due to the number of drugs in his small body. There is nothing for me to do but sit here next to him and wait, wait for the doctors to come up with some new plan or treatment. An almost crushing sense of despair and doom weighs down on me. My son is dying, and my friend is on trial before the whole world.

The situation with Denim Guy has played out exactly as he predicted. Nearly every country in the world has investigated him. It has been determined to haul him to The Hague where he is to face the charges. From back channels I have learned the charges, numbering in the hundreds, will be condensed down to ten categories.

Camera angles shift between Denim Guy, the prosecutor, and the judge. Denim Guy has chosen to represent himself.

"Is the ... is the mic on?" asks the judge to someone off-camera. "Yes. Good morning, everyone. Madam Court Officer, can you please mention the case?"

"Good morning, Your Honor." The court officer nods to the judge. "This is the situation in all 123 Countries of the States Parties to the Rome Statute, and an additional non-Party state from six continents et al., in the case of The Prosecutor versus Yeshua bar Yosef, aka The Forever Man, case reference ICC-31/10-01/67. And for the record, we are in open session."

"Thank you." The judge adjusts his glasses and shuffles some papers. "Can I ask the parties to introduce themselves, starting with the prosecution?"

A blond man in formal court dress stands up. "Good morning, Your Honor. Good morning, everyone. My name is Anton Curel, appearing for the prosecution today. With me, trial lawyer Jeannette Le Fleur; associate trial lawyers, Margaret Stein, Jeffrey Billings, Surat Meta; associate legal officer, Angelique Berg; case manager, Faith Perez; and intern Otto Hein. Thank you."

"Thank you very much, Mr. Curel. And for the defense please." "Your Honor," now Denim Guy stands up. "Good morning, everyone in and around the courtroom. I am Yeshua bar Yosef, otherwise known as Jesus of Nazareth, The Forever Man, King of Kings and Lord of Lords, Son of God and Son of Man, the First and Last, the Bread of Life, The Creator, and the Messiah."

The judge looks at Denim Guy over his glasses. "Very well. Good morning to you Mr. Forever Man. For the record, is this your preferred nomenclature?"

"That is fine, if it pleases the court." Denim Guy sits down.

"And I am to understand you wish to conduct your defense. If so, could you please confirm this fact, that you would like to conduct your own defense in person without any counsel? Over to you, Mr. Forever Man."

Presiding Judge Mathieu lists off the rules and procedures for this pre-trial hearing and ensures everyone speaks and responds slowly to assist the interpreters.

Denim Guy stands again. He adjusts the mic. "Your Honor, I wish to confirm that on the 28th, which is today, I signed a waiver for legal assistance for the duration of the proceedings."

"Yes, that's what we heard. It's your right of course. Quickly, because I have forgotten, please state your date of birth and nationality."

"I am an Israeli citizen. I was born on September 17th, 2 BC." The courtroom breaks out into laughter.

Judge Mathieu bangs his gavel. "Order, please. Order! Knock it off." The room goes silent. "If you can't keep quiet then I will have you removed. Thank you, Mr. Forever Man. Now, let me start by saying that this Court is governed by the Assembly of States Parties, which is made up of the states that are party to the Rome Statute. Given the uniqueness of the case, the omniscient characteristics of the individual in question, and the number of offenses, the Assembly has amended the articles of the Rome Statue to grant emergency powers to me for this specific case. Whereas the investigative portion of the case has taken place over the last ten months and has been completed, and whereas a pre-trial phase would normally precede the trial, I have chosen to execute these new powers bestowed upon me by the Assembly and combine the pre-trial and trial hearings into one hearing, with a summary judgment and sentencing later today."

Surprised murmurs break out in the court room.

"But Your Honor," Denim Guy pleads. "How can this be fair?" Bang! Bang! Bang! Judge Mathieu slams the gavel down. "Silence.

The court's decision is final. Subsequently, a confirmation of charges hearing will be bypassed pursuant to the provisions of the Rome Statute for this case as well as certain rights of the suspect, Mr. Forever Man, which have been amended given his confirmed … abilities."

Denim Guy stands. "Your Honor, may I—"

"No, you may not. You will have a chance to speak, but first, per Article 60 of the Rome Statute, I would like to ask you whether you have been informed of the charges against you and in the instant case, the offences against the administration of justice as defined and outlined in the amended Article 70 of the Rome Statute. So, I am going to ask, so that you have a specific idea of the matters with which you are charged, I'm going to ask the courtroom to read out the offences against the administration of justice with which you are charged, and which have been outlined in the official warrant of arrest on 10 June 2036. Madam Courtroom Officer, could you please read out these offences to us."

"Thank you, Your Honor." The court officer opens a folder and clears her throat. "Count 1: CRIMES OF AGGRESSION, The Forever Man is criminally responsible under Article 8 as a direct perpetrator for the planning and direct exercise of control over a State or States, including the entire continents of Europe and Asia, when, in the country of Ukraine, The Forever Man forced the physical movement of these countries through the creation of a new mountain range, incurring a change in location of these countries against their will, thus violating their sovereignty."

Denim Guy raises his cuffed hands. "Your Honor, that was to save lives—"

"Ancillary charges," the court officer continues. "Pursuant to the amended Articles, nine counts incorporated herein involving offenses in violation of Party and Non-Party States."

"How is this possible?" Denim Guy asks.

Judge Mathieu slams his gavel. "The suspect in question will remain silent while the charges are read. Madam Court Officer, please continue, and for the sake of brevity you may dispense with the statute citations."

"Count 2: ILLEGAL MINING, under jurisdiction of the European Union, The Forever Man is criminally responsible as a direct perpetrator when the offence was committed during the aforementioned mountain-raising event on the border of Ukraine and Russia."

"Count 3: UNLAWFUL USE OF PORTS, under established Maritime Law, The Forever Man is criminally responsible as a direct perpetrator when, in the same event, ports of harbor were illegally moved without permission."

"Count 4: SMUGGLING AND HARBORING ALIENS, under United States jurisdiction, The Forever Man is criminally responsible as a direct perpetrator, when, on the 28th of April he illegally transported aliens across the US—Mexico border without first arriving at a port of entry."

"Seeking asylum is a human right," Denim Guy mutters, his head bowed.

"Silence," Judge Mathieu commands. "Last warning Mr. Forever Man, next time I will hold you in contempt. Go on, Madam Court Officer."

"Count 5: IMPROPER ENTRY BY AN ALIEN ..."

The list goes on and I can hardly believe my ears. This once-hallowed institution has now become a kangaroo court. Count 6: PROVIDING MATERIAL SUPPOR TO TERRORISTS, this comes supposedly from when The Forever Man stopped the Israeli military incursion into Jenin Refugee Camp. Count 7: FORGING LEGAL DOCUMENTS, a charge directed at the clerical error on his passport regarding his birthdate.

From here the charges became even more absurd. Count 8: ENVIRONMENTAL TERRORISM, a war crime for the orchestration of the manna falling from the sky and the supposed distress it caused on people and the local ecology. For the same event

Denim Guy was charged with Count 9: IMPROPER FOOD STORAGE, because the manna fell from the sky and wasn't stored according to international regulation, and Count 10: CLEAN WATER ACT VIOLATIONS, a charge made because the springs that Forever Man caused to come forth in areas of drought for the purpose of drinking were not tested for chemicals by local authorities.

"Thank you, Madam Court Officer," says the judge. "Mr. Forever Man, have you heard the charges?"

"I have heard the charges."

"Very good." The judge turns to the defense. He reads to Denim Guy his rights and asks if he understands.

"I understand," he responds.

"Let it be recorded that Mr. Forever Man understands the charges. Now, having weighed all the evidence, I have determined there is enough merit to the charges to advance to trial. Mr. Forever Man, how do you plead?"

"I make no plea."

"Mr. Forever Man, you must tell the court your plea. Guilty or not guilty?"

Denim Guy says nothing.

"Very well. In that case, we shall conclude the pre-trial hearing, and commence the trial. Forthwith, the Mr. Forever Man shall now be referred to as the accused. Mr. Curel, you may present your case."

The prosecutor stands. "Thank you, Your Honor. We believe this is an open-and-shut case, Your Honor. We have ample video evidence of the crimes committed, we also have a firsthand witness in a Mr. Ethan Tellinger, a journalist with the *Times*, whose articles documented the words, actions, plans, intentions, and state of mind of the accused."

Sam's EKG monitor beeps as I bury my face in my hands. "Oh, no. They're using my article against Denim Guy."

The articles are entered into the record. Audio from my phone is played for the courtroom. Did they hack my phone? How in the world did they get those recordings? A light bulb flickers on inside my brain: the bizarre interrogation at the *Times* headquarters and the government agents, those *Visitors from the Shadow World*. One of them left during the interview. Which one was it? Mr. Legg? The creepy dude said he was going to the restroom, did he not? He must've done something to my phone while he was out. Talk about a violation of privacy, but what other explanation could there be? What other time could the government have tapped into my phone? It had to be him.

"Lastly," says the smirking prosecutor. "We have on record the admission of The Forever Man that he committed these acts, and that his all-knowing nature indicates he knew he was violating these laws, that he was acting with criminal intent. The crimes were documented in real-time to the public. We believe this documentation, the firsthand witness, and the deified nature of the accused prove, beyond a reasonable doubt, that the accused is guilty."

Curel then spends the next hour presenting the prosecution's evidence for each of the ten counts. My articles are referenced repeatedly, as well as the video evidence from the media, and interviews from people with whom Denim Guy has interacted. At the end of the hour the prosecutor rests his case. Judge Mathieu turns to Denim Guy.

"Mr. Forever Man," he says. "You have the right to say nothing, or you can mount a defense. It's up to you."

Denim Guy stands. "Last time I was on Trial, I was accused before Pilate. I did not defend myself then, but this time I will. This time I will speak to your hearts and address these charges."

"It's your choice. Let's take a fifteen-minute break, then, when we reconvene, you can proceed with your defense." Judge Mathieu exits the courtroom. After he leaves, the court attendees stand up and stretch their legs.

Forty-five minutes later Judge Mathieu gavels in the hearing. I expect to hear Denim Guy give his defense, but instead the judge goes on a long soliloquy about arcane rules and procedures, citing various statutes and precedents. It all sounds like gobbledygook to justify the outrageous and unjust nature of the proceedings. Sure, The Forever Man was a unique individual, but does that excuse this shambolic hearing? Not to mention the violation of privacy concerning my phone. If I received a subpoena, I would have complied of course. I would have turned over whatever possessions of mine they wanted, but no, they didn't even ask, they just hacked my phone, or were given access to it by the phone manufacturer. I'm not sure which is worse.

"Having established these legal justifications," says the judge. "And explained how these proceedings will take place, I will now turn it over to the accused so that he may offer his defense. You may proceed, Mr. Forever Man."

The *accused* stands. Before he begins, Denim Guy closes his eyes, and his lips move in silence as if he is saying a prayer.

Judge Mathieu stifles a yawn. "Come on Mr. Forever Man, we don't have all day."

Denim Guy opens his eyes. "During the last trial, some two thousand years ago, I was not masculine enough for the people. They wanted Barabbas, a fighter, a zealot, a charismatic, a fiery leader to punish enemies and lead a rebellion. I, on the other hand, was too passive for them. Now, in this age, I am too active for you. In both ages the problem is the same. It is your heart. Whether the year is 36 AD, or 2036 AD, people and governments are threatened by me.

"Since I have returned, my message then was the same as it is now. It is a message of non-violence and peace and love and gentleness, but also forgiveness and faithfulness and righteous judgment. My purpose is not to defend myself, at least not in the way that you expect. The charges that have been brought forward are technically valid according to the letter of the law. However, it is to the spirit of the law that I will address. Even so, on technicality there are flaws with the prosecution. As to the first count, no border of any country was changed, save for the Baltic states who gave me permission to act, and the border of Russia, the aggressor state.

"For Count 2 of illegal mining, this law only applies to land belonging to sovereign nations. The mountains I caused to come forth are, in fact, new land from under the surface of the earth, and not belonging to any country. So, as you can see, no violation has taken place. Count 2 must be thrown out. It does not apply.

"Count 3 is disputable. It is true the ports geospatial coordinates changed, but their position relative to their location within their country did not change. No harm was done, and the action saved millions of lives.

"As to counts 4 and 5, these laws were given to ensure order and safety, which was my purpose in bringing the migrants across the border at the location of my choosing. To make the children wait for days in the heat at an approved customs checkpoint would be an injustice and a greater crime than crossing the border at a place without a port of entry. I cannot act unjustly. A just action supersedes flawed human interpretations and intentions of law. This is the spirit of all law, which, in and of itself, cannot account for specific circumstances, thus, exceptions can be made, and are made, even by this court. Even so, according to international law one does not have to go through a port of entry to enter a country if one is seeking asylum. Seeking asylum is a human right.

"Count 6 should be dismissed because no proof can be given that *tangible* support of terrorism was given. The IDF did not have to abandon their military operation, I simply convinced them this was the best course of action because a boy had already been injured.

"Count 7 should also be thrown out because I did not knowingly forge anything, nor could you ever prove such. The mistake on my passport was an honest coding error.

"The same applies to Count 8. There is no proof any of my miracles, signs, or wonders constitute an act of eco-terrorism. No one has been harmed. The environment has not been adversely affected. In fact, since I returned the climate has stabilized, CO_2 emissions have decreased, flora and fauna have flourished, species that were once on the brink of extinction are now beginning to thrive.

"On Count 9, I will admit to improperly storing manna if a single person can suggest to me *how* one should properly store food from heaven. Perhaps we should call an expert from the Food and Drug Administration? The same goes for Count 10. If a single scientist or government agency can prove the spring water is contaminated, then I will admit guilt. But you have already tested the water, no? You have the results, so why didn't you present that as part of your case Mr. Curel? I tell you why. It is because the water is purer than the bottled water you have on your desk.

"This trial is a farce. You would have no power over me, save for the power that was given to you from above … by me. All authority on heaven and earth has been given to me. I am the One who changes the times and the seasons. I set up rulers and I remove rulers. Before the foundation of the world, I established the table of nations, including the nations of this age, and the age to come. I alone sit at the right hand of the Father, and it is I alone who judge the nations. It was your intent to judge me, but, in fact, it is I who have come here to judge you.

"My judgment is pure and good and just. Did you feed the hungry? Did you welcome the stranger? Did you clothe the naked, care for the sick, defend the defenseless, do justice for the poor, visit the prisoner, and promote the health of the environment? Indeed, you have not. I know this because what you have done to these you have also done to me. You did not feed the hungry, you exploited the hungry. For ill-gotten gain you gave them expensive harmful food to eat, and poison to drink. They naked lie in your streets, and do you clothe them? No, you throw them in jail. You also do not heal the sick. For the love of money, you ignore science. When people do need care, you saddle them with debts they cannot repay. And the strangers and refugees who come to you for help? You exclude them and treat them like dogs, less than human. For the poor, you instituted systems of oppression and racism so they would stay poor. And this beautiful planet, did you manage it well, as I told you to do in the Garden of Eden? No, you have abused it for your own selfish desires. You corrupt, and lie, and oppress. You lift up the rich and powerful, and step on the necks of the weak. By my grace alone have the salt of the earth refined you, yet still you resist correction. You thought of the poor as your footstool, your laughingstock. But they are your judge! I have come back to the world to be victorious over the darkness, to reclaim the lost and sinners so they can enter the fullness of God. I am a Redeemer. This is my work, to redeem all of creation to myself, and I stand in judgment against the nations."

Denim Guy turns to the Judge. "Your Honor, the defense rests."

Judge Mathieu exhales deeply. "Very well, Mr. Curel do you have a closing statement?"

"Yes, Your Honor." The Prosecutor steps around the table. "If what the accused says is true, then we are put in a difficult position. Do we uphold the law and convict God as a criminal, or do we ignore the law for the most powerful? This has always been the test of Lady Justice. Will we have one rule for the weak, and one rule for the poor? No law for God, but laws for the rest of us? The accused says he has come here to do good, but can this really be possible? How can we function as a society with *him* here? God, present with us on earth doesn't make things better, it makes things more complicated. It doesn't bring order, it brings disorder. So, what do we do? Stop having elections? Throw out democracy, embrace authoritarianism just because he's here? Think about this. He claims he is innocent, but if he really is all-knowing and all-powerful, then he *knew* he would end up here. When he did all those great miracles and wonders, when he helped save all those lives, he *knew* he was breaking our laws and that he would be convicted. This proves his state of mind … and it proves his guilt! Your honor, the prosecution rests."

"Thank you, Mr. Prosecutor. Mr. Forever Man, the floor is yours if you wish to make a closing statement."

Denim Guy pauses. "You wonder how you will govern with me here. I will tell you. No longer will you govern with impunity or injustice. You will govern with accountability. You will go on like you did before. You will hold your elections and pass your laws and do all the things that governments do. But perhaps now you will be a bit wiser. You will know the government rests on *my* shoulders. I am not here to destroy you. I am here to judge you, and my judgment is love. You call me the accused, but who is the accuser? I have nothing else to say, Your Honor."

"Very well," Judge Mathieu whispers to the other judges on the panel. They confer in hushed tones. There's a lot of head nodding.

Judge Mathieu comes back to the mic. "This concludes the pre-trial, trial, and closing statements. I would like to thank both teams, the prosecution and defense. The Chamber wishes to thank also the registry for the support and help throughout this trial, and that would include everyone in and outside of this courtroom. I appreciate the interpreters, transcribers, and court officers. I also greatly appreciate the VWU and many more. I thank my officers and legal team. I must say I enjoyed this trial very much. The Chamber will now retire and … retire to do our deliberation as required of us under the emergency provisions of the amended Article 74 of the Rome Statute. We will reconvene in one hour."

I flip off the TV and rub my eyes. My gut tells me Denim Guy is screwed. I had covered hearings at the International Criminal Court before and every part of what I just witnessed was bizarre. The prosecutor did bring up a valid concern. It's much easier to order society when God is an idea. When God becomes a physical reality things become much more … *complicated*. Was the world ready for this kind of reality? Humanity was now in uncharted waters. The first Jesus didn't insert himself into government like he is doing now. I sure hope Denim Guy knows what he is doing. Knowing him, he probably does.

TWENTY-THREE
AWAKENINGS

Barnes Jewish Hospital, St. Louis, MO June 29th, 2036

I'M AWAKENED NEXT TO Sam by an alert on my phone. The Forever Man has been found guilty of all charges. He has been sentenced to life in prison. How do you sentence someone to life in prison who lives forever? I don't have much time to think about it. Another alert pops up on my phone, this time with a video. I click the link. A web page opens a video of Denim Guy in the courtroom breaking apart his handcuffs and ankle chains like they're made of Lego. He says something but the audio is unclear, and then … well, and then, he disappears. Literally just … *poof.* Gone.

Sam begins to wake up. "Water," he croaks.

I put my phone down and grab the cup of water from the nightstand. I place the straw in his mouth. All his strength is needed just to lift his head and take a few drinks. Gently, he lays his head back down. I adjust his teddy bear so it's secured under his arm. Sam loves his teddy.

A man in a white coat walks into the room. "Ethan?" asks Dr. Jayapal.

"Yes?"

"Could we speak outside the room for a moment?"

The tone in his voice said it all. My legs are like stone weights as I follow him to a private waiting room at the other end of the cancer ward.

"Please have a seat," says the doctor.

I sit down with an incredible feeling of doom. I hate this room. I hate the wallpaper and the carpet and the chairs and the fluorescent lighting. I've seen other families come in here. The opaque tones of the decorations remind me of a funeral parlor.

Dr. Jayapal clicks his pen and secures it in his coat pocket. "So, I've been consulting with our staff here, other doctors, and a few oncology experts around the country. At this point, we believe all the options have been explored and perhaps it might just be time to make Sam as comfortable as possible."

"Wait, what are you saying? Move Sam into hospice?" "As I said, at this point it's probably—"

"No, no, no. I'm not giving up. No one is giving up, understand? There must be some kind of treatment, or chemo drug, a new experimental treatment, something, anything. We just, we can't give up, not yet."

Dr. Jayapal sighs. "Ethan, we have investigated everything. Yes, there are other types of experimental treatments but none that would benefit Sam and his unique situation. The cancer cells adapt to whatever we throw at it. Unfortunately, at this time, we simply don't have the methods to treat a rare cancer like this."

I punch the wall. "That's not good enough!" The doctor stares at the floor.

"Do something!" I scream at him. My phone beeps. The app alerts me to Sam's vital signs. I stick the phone in Dr. Jayapal's face. "Look! He's alive! His heart is beating. He's still fighting! Why aren't you fighting?"

"Ethan—"

"You don't even care, do you? What is this, just another Tuesday for you, right? On to the next patient, huh?"

"How about I refer you to someone else for a second opinion." "Someone else? You just said you already talked with everyone!" "Yes,

I did. And another oncologist is probably going to tell you the same thing. We have reached a point where our goals have to change. In this moment, what's best for Sam may not be curing the disease, but instead, maximizing quality of life."

"Quality of life?" I grab the doctor by the coat and haul him to his feet. "You mean death, that's what you mean. Death. I will not prepare my son to die."

"You need to think about Sam's comfort. Hospice does not mean he will stop receiving treatment, it means the treatment he will receive will be palliative. The cancer has run its course. We cannot reverse the damage that has been done. Initially, we were encouraged by the result of the new chemo, but the prognosis never changed. It was always twelve to eighteen months."

I let go of Dr. Jayapal and collapse in a chair.

"You are welcome to stay here as long as you need, but Sam's organs are shutting down. In the next few days, we will most likely have to put Sam on life support."

Dr. Jayapal keeps talking, but I've stopped listening. My mind simply cannot accept what he is saying, so instead, it races around my skull looking for a solution, a way out of this never-ending nightmare. The waiting room suddenly gets wobbly. I realize I'm experiencing vertigo. The urge to vomit roils in my belly and up into my throat. I stumble to the bathroom and empty my stomach.

Hard to believe, but at this moment, I wish he was here. Denim Guy. He always knew what to say, and what to do. Figures. The moment I actually need him the most is the moment he isn't around. Typical. But that was life. In the end, you are on your own and no one is there to help.

Feeling numb, I walk back to Sam's room. I kiss his forehead and think about all the fun things a healthy kid should be doing right now, all the things Sam has missed out on. It just wasn't fair. Why Sam? Why did it have to be my son that suffered this? Why did he have to be the one who didn't get to experience the thrill of a roller coaster, the fun of a playground, the joy of friends, prom, graduation, the love of a mother, falling in love, marriage, becoming a father? All of it, all of life robbed from him.

I lay my head next to Sam. "I haven't given up, buddy. I'm still fighting. I'll never give up fighting for you." I curl up into a ball and drift off to sleep.

The next day is much the same. Sam barely moves. He sleeps all day. Nurses come in and out, pumping him full of drugs. I rarely see the doctor. For myself, I can't stand the sight of food, or anything of comfort. Sam no longer eats, so I don't eat. It just doesn't seem right. The days drag on, I realize my son is already in palliative care. All they are doing is managing the pain. On my phone I flip through pictures of us. The deterioration in his health, even from a few weeks ago, is noticeable. Sam is wasting away, dying before my eyes. Bones protrude from his face.

Fear and despair are ever-present. Mostly, I just feel anger. No, not anger, rage. Pure rage. I rage at the nurses and the doctors. I read Sam jokes from his favorite joke book. I talk to him, sing to him, hold his hand. On my phone I do research. I call clinics in Texas and California. I call doctors at St. Jude's and the Mayo Clinic. The answer is always the same: too late, nothing we can do, just make him comfortable. I have come to hate that word, comfortable. To me, it just means death. Weeks later Sam is intubated. His lungs are shutting down, one by one. They hook him up to other life-support machines. At one point, Sam opens his eyes. He looks at me like a stranger. My own boy doesn't even recognize his dad. If it wasn't for Teddy, Sam would be all alone in a room surrounded by machines. I begin to doubt myself, maybe Dr. Jayapal was right. Maybe I should have just moved him in to hospice. Then he could die in his room, not with all this scary medical stuff around. At this moment I'm just dragging it out, torturing my son.

Day after day this goes on, until one morning in August I am awoken on the hospital room floor by Dr. Jayapal.

"Ethan," he says, nudging my shoulder. "Wake up, Ethan."

Rubbing my eyes, I sit up. "What is it? What's going on?"

"It's OK." The doctor helps me to my feet. "Perhaps we could talk about Sam."

"How is he doing?"

"Ethan, Sam is brain-dead. There is no longer any activity. The only thing keeping him alive is the intubation and ECMO. It's up to you, but at this point, we don't want to prolong Sam's suffering. You need to start thinking about when Sam should be taken off life-support."

I walk over to the bed. My poor Sam is unrecognizable, a husk, covered in tubes and wires. What am I doing to my son? Tears blur my vision.

"OK." I look up at the doctor. "Turn it off." My hands fold around Sam's little hand.

The doctor gives instructions to the nurses. The next seconds pass like a dream. Life-support machines alarm as they no longer sense any life, the medical staff have removed the tubes, and IVs, and wires. The machines are shut down, but there's still one alarm going off. It's my phone letting me know it can no longer read Sam's pulse. I dismiss the notification and then the grief hits me.

Unaware of how long I sit there weeping, eventually I realize I'm the only one in the room with Sam. I look at my boy. My beautiful boy, he seems so peaceful now. Not sure what to do, I decide to go outside and get some air. The elevator takes me down to the lobby. I find a bench next to a flowering Cleveland Pear tree and cry some more. Vaguely, I notice the shadows of people walking by. Someone finally stops. I look up and recognize a pair of faded jeans.

"He's gone," I say to Denim Guy. "My boy is dead."

Denim Guy put an arm around me. His compassionate touch angers me.

"Where have you been?" I demand. "Why weren't you here?"

"Ethan—"

"No, Sam didn't have to die. So, what's your excuse?" I stand up and push Denim Guy in the chest. "You could have saved him! Why didn't you do anything?" I clench my fist and strike Denim Guy in the face. He staggers backward. "God damn you! God damn you, God!"

He edges back towards me. The weeks of grief and stress crush my soul. I collapse into his arms and weep.

"What's your excuse?" My fists pound against his chest. "Where is Vivian? Why didn't you save her? Why didn't you save Sam. Why did you take my family away? Well? What do you have to say? Say something." I push away and look him in the eye. "Say something God damnit!"

Denim Guy meets my accusing gaze eye for eye. "Ask me," he whispers. "That's what I have to say, and what I've said all along. Ask me."

"No, I can't, I ca—"

"Ask me, Ethan. What have you got to lose?"

I think about it for second. "Will you say yes?"

He wraps his arms around me. "You have to ask."

I weep like a blubbering child. I miss them so much. What did I have to lose? I realize now, either I must ask, or I must die. I can feel myself giving in, and as I give in, that burden on my shoulders, a burden I didn't know was there, it started to feel lighter. Yes, I give up. I give up everything. I give up my pride. I give up my anger. I give up my doubt. I give up my dreams. I give up my pain. I give up Vivian. I give up Sam. I give up.

"All right," I say in between sobs. "Fine. You win. Will you—" My phone dings with a new notification. I know the sound as Sam's vital signs app. I back away from Denim Guy and look at his face. He stands there looking at me, the same all-knowing expression on his face. My phone alerts with another notification.

"Don't you mess with me," I say pointing at him. "What is this? What did you do?"

Exhaling, I get out my phone and look at the screen. I look at Denim Guy. I look back at my phone, my hands trembling. "Wha … what is happening?"

"Hey, Ethan," Denim Guy puts his hands in his pockets. He looks up to the window of Sam's room. "You should probably go back inside now."

Staring at my phone, I back up to the sliding doors, seriously wondering if I'm hallucinating. I turn and break out into a run. I sprint through the lobby. Frantically, I push the button for the elevator. It opens and I push the button for the third-floor cancer ward.

"Come on! Move!" I shout at the elevator. My finger bangs on the third floor button over and over and over again.

The door opens. I run down the hall. I turn left and keeping running. Halfway down the corridor my knees buckle. There's a healthy, normal-looking boy in a hospital gown standing in the doorway of Sam's room. He's holding a teddy bear.

The boy sees me and smiles. "Hi, Dad."

TWENTY-FOUR
THE NEW WORLD

Allerton Park, Monticello, IL October 9th, 2037

THE SCENE IS LIKE a painting. Denim Guy and Sam are flying a kite in the sprawling fourteen-acre meadow of Allerton Park. I recline in the grass and watch the butterfly-shaped kite fly in the wind against a backdrop of blue sky and puffy white clouds. It all feels vaguely familiar, but I can't quite put my finger on why it seems like I've been here before.

A year later and I still can't believe my son is here, alive, running around and playing, flying a kite with his new best friend … Jesus of Nazareth. Sam breaks out into laughter as Denim Guy runs up a hill with the kite string.

Since Sam came back to life—well, I suppose I should call it what it is—since Sam's *resurrection* the world had begun to change. People began to get healthier. Hospital populations decreased. The number of sick and dying all over the planet basically vanished over the course of the year. Injuries were also down to nothing. Generally speaking, accidents had nearly become non-existent, and what accidents did happen resulted in no injuries. War and conflict were at historic lows, with projections that in the next five years there would be no war anywhere for the first time in human history. There were also no natural disasters, no animal attacks, the earth's population was booming. As great as this was, it also caused a little bit of turmoil. Apparently, about 10% of the world economy was healthcare. Now that everyone was getting healthy and not getting injured, there was now the beginnings of an economic realignment away from medicine. Hospitals were closing, their rooms permanently vacant and their clinics empty because there was no demand for them. Even the aged were getting stronger, younger. Those with mental illness were experiencing what can only be described as a mass mental healing and rejuvenation.

Enmity and strife between people groups had also nearly disappeared or would be gone by the end of the year. There seemed to be a change in mood. People no longer argued on social media. Sure, there were disagreements, as there always is, but now it was different. Now, people had started to tolerate and appreciate their differences. Partisanship was at an all-time low. Hatred had melted away. Antisemitic chat rooms and conspiracy theorists took down their websites. Systems of oppression and racism were acknowledged, and steps taken to amend what was wrong and unjust. People no longer sought their own advantage, but rather, the advantage of their neighbor. They no longer asked for money, they asked for forgiveness. Governments amended their budgets away from defense spending because there was no need for weapons of war. All within a year, there was grace in the world.

Many didn't believe it would last. Most attributed it to The Forever Man, but not all. Some blamed science, or human progress, or whatever religion or God they worshipped. Today, seeing my cancer-stricken once-dead son now healthy and living, I know the truth.

Sam plants the kite spool in the ground. He jumps on Denim Guy's back, and together they come sit down next to me.

"Did you see it, Dad?" Sam asks. "He made the wind blow faster!"

I ruffle his blond hair. "Oh, is that what happened?" I look over at Denim Guy, who gives me a wink. "Pretty cool, huh?"

"Yeah. Denim Guy can do anything. And he's my best friend."

"Mine too."

We lay on our backs in the grass and watch the clouds pass by above us. Each of us take turns calling out their shapes. We see a castle, a dog, a dragon, a lady, and a car.

Suddenly, Denim Guy sits up. "Well, it's about that time." "Oh? Time for what?" I ask.

"Time to go for a walk." Denim Guy points to the gardens. "How about we start over there."

We leave the kite staked in the ground and head toward two limestone pillars with twenty-four-inch stone lions on top. They mark the entrance to the carefully manicured gardens of Allerton Park and demarcate a long expanse of formal garden walkway. From there we walk the Triangle Parterre Garden connecting the east portion with the Annual Garden to the west. Arborvitae line the sidewalk, giving it a closed-in appearance. At the end of the path are two more columns, each topped with Assyrian Lions.

Limestone models of The Three Graces are next seen on the right. The three statues, in Greek mythology - Aglaia, Thalia, and Euphrosyne – personified beauty, charm, and grace. To the left is the annual garden with the statue of the Marble Faun. Next is a seven-foot copy of Auguste Rodin's Adam sculpture. Beyond this statue is a garden of over 1600 peony flowers with 68 varieties, located on the north side of the main walkway. On the south side is the Bulb Garden, where there are 105 rows of narcissus, varieties of lilies, and white Siberian iris.

Sam runs around and explores the garden, I walk with Denim Guy, neither of us saying much. We pass through the Chinese Parterre Garden and the Avenue of the Chinese Musicians, eventually descending a series of steps and into the Sunken Garden. Designed as the finale to the formal gardens, this architectural garden was unusual, with no central path, and surrounded by elevated turf and hemlocks inside the upper wall. Both ends of the garden have modern stairways in the art deco style with pylons topped by gilded Japanese Guardian Fish. The stairs lead to the upper-level walls which are lattice work with vines growing up and hanging down.

We explore this area, noting the unusual echo the shape of the garden causes our voices to make when we stand on the stairs.

Moseying onward, we hit a small trail and eventually the road leading westward toward the Garden of the Sun Singer.

A car drives by, and I grab Sam to move him out of the way.

"It will take some getting used to," says Denim Guy. "This new Sam."

"What do you mean?"

"His new body. It is immortal, Ethan. Sam cannot be injured. He will mature into a man, but he will never grow old, never get sick, never die. His cells will never decay, nor can they be damaged."

"Yeah, that will take some getting used to."

"In other words, his body is like my body. Indestructible and incorruptible. You will have to teach him how to carry himself. As weak as he once was, Sam was perfectly suited to be *him*."

"Him? Him who?"

"The Second Born of the Dead."

I exhale, trying to take all this in. "So, it's true then. Sam is the one you were talking about before in Somalia, the one who will start the Awakening.

"Correct."

"And what exactly is this *Awakening* going to be?"

He smiles. "You didn't know it then, but I did."

My arm goes around Denim Guy. "Ah, more riddles. You didn't answer my question."

Denim Guy smiles. "I could tell you, yes, but I'd rather show you."

"Oh fine, have it your way. So, when is this Awakening going to happen?"

The road opens into the clearing where stands the statue of the Sun Singer. A few people mill about on the grass taking pictures. So many memories of this place. The best and worst moments of my life happened right here.

"Right now," says Denim Guy stopping on the road. He turns to face me. "I searched the earth for faith, a piece of bread cast upon the waters. After many days, I found it in you, Ethan." He nods toward the statue of the Sun Singer. "It's happening now. Look and see for yourself."

My eyes follow where he is pointing. Sun rays filter through the arms of the Sun Singer. I shield my eyes from the light. "I don't see anything."

"Look closer."

"Where? I can't ..."

I forget whatever it is I am about to say. I see her now. A woman sitting on a blanket in the grass, writing in a book. She's wearing a white dress, her auburn hair pulled back into a ponytail over one shoulder. The woman sets down her book. Smiling, she turns to me.

Denim Guy steadies me as I nearly faint.

Sam pulls at my hand. "Dad? Who's that lady? Do you know her?" Drying my cheeks, I take a knee. "Sammy, that's your mom."

Sam's eyes widen with excitement. He pulls away from me, but then stops, unsure if he should keep going.

"It's all right," I say. "Go on, she's waiting for you."

He takes off running toward the woman in white. She runs toward him. They embrace on the exact same spot I cursed God and swore never to pray again. In the sky above the Sun Singer, I hear voices, like a great choir bursting into song. Little points of light appear, people with shining faces, robed in white, are descending out of the heavens. I turn to Denim Guy. "Is that ... are those ...? Is this it? Is this the Awakening?"

Denim Guy doesn't hear my question. He is looking up to the heavens. "As it is written: *Your dead shall live. Their bodies will rise. You who dwell in the dust awake and sing for joy.*"

"How? Where—?"

"BUNGI-TIME," he replies with an amused smile. He places a hand on my shoulder. "Look, Ethan, we have an eternity for questions and answers. Right now, your family is waiting for you. Go to them."

Denim Guy turns me around. At last, it all makes sense. Every hurt and pain. Every prayer. Every doubt. Every tear. Every particle. Every chemical reaction. Every moment of laughter. Everything he told me. Every word. In this moment, all his riddles and teachings are made clear by the image of a mother reunited with her child in the Garden of the Sun Singer.

They're calling me to join them. I start running …

The End.

www.ingramcontent.com/pod-product-compliance
Lightning Source LLC
LaVergne TN
LVHW042253070526
838201LV00106B/305/J